MY DRAGON MATE

Broken Souls 3

ALISA WOODS

Cover by BZN Studio

ISBN: 9781693768743

My Dragon Mate (**Broken Souls 3**)

When dark elves corrupt the very thing you are, there's only one path to redemption.

This is all my fault.

The fates sent them to me in a dream—the twin soul mates and the dragon man with the pale brown eyes. I knew they were key to everything. I knew I'd pay a price for it.

What I didn't see coming was the flutter in my belly when the dragon man's eyes were upon me.

He's a fine thing, but that's not important—rescuing these women from the feckin' Elves. *That's* important.

Not least because it's my fault they're here.

Witches are supposed to be healers. Matchmakers of dragons. My mother and her mother before her… we aren't supposed to be destroyers.

So I'll undo what I've done, but I tell myself, *There's nothing more for you, Alice.*

Don't let that dragon man wreck your head… or all your carefully laid plans.

Alice's a witch held hostage. Constantine's a dragon who gave up long ago… together they might save dragonkind, but it could already be too late for their broken souls.

My Dragon Mate is a steamy new dragon shifter romance that'll heat up the sheets with love and warm your heart with dragonfire.

ONE

Constantine

THIS SHRUNKEN MAN BEFORE ME IS MY FATE.

I know this as surely as I am dragon.

I sit by Grigore's bedside, waiting for him to awaken. Just a few weeks ago, we were down in New York City, scouting for the fiery women who might be soul mates for a dragon somewhere. Grigore's soul was tired of the search, even then, but that fatigue hadn't yet manifested in the withering of his body. Now, the slow death of despair has sped up. His hair is gone. His skin is wrinkled. The artificial youth of our magic has fled. He could have only hours left, maybe days—no longer than a week.

The entire lair will take turns keeping him company until the end.

Grigore moves in his sleep, a rattle deep in his chest surfacing as a cough—but his eyes remain closed. He's barely a hundred years old, which is alarming. If the younger dragons lose hope, there is none for any of us. Even less for me, but then I gave up two centuries ago—now I hunt only for the others, hoping to find them mates before it's too late. Before they're lying on a hospital bed, wheezing their last breaths.

Grigore coughs again, but this time he wakes. His bleary gaze is pinned to the ceiling.

"Hey." I take his hand and squeeze it, letting him know I'm here. "It's my turn to babysit your ass."

He smiles—it's a mockery of the panty-dropping smile he deployed with me on our hunts. "You drew the short straw, huh?" He slowly, with apparent great effort, turns his head toward me. The pristine white pillow barely dents under its weight. "Did you kill the witch?"

"No." But relief washes through me that he still remembers—loss of memory means they're near the end. Yet I wince inside. I'd hoped to avoid this particular topic. "I spared her. Turns out, she might be able to help us."

"Spared her?" Grigore's smile twists into a smirk. "Or got your ass kicked again?"

"Little of both."

He laughs, but it quickly turns into a hacking cough. I grip his hand through it, supporting him as the convulsions lift him from the bed. Finally, it settles, and I ease him back down.

"*Fuck,*" he wheezes. "Don't make me laugh."

"Well, there goes all my material."

He smiles again, but his eyes are drifting closed. "Save your material for the ladies."

"Always." That's my one useful purpose— romancing women into that first True Kiss, and maybe into bed, then seducing them into running the gauntlet of my dragon brothers, on the remote chance they might find their mate. But seeing Grigore is gutting me —not just because his fate is mine, and possibly every other dragon on earth, but because there's suddenly a glimmer of hope on the horizon, something that might save many of us… and it came too late for him.

Grigore sighs. There's so much weariness in it. "Tell me about the witch." His eyes are fully closed now. His breathing settles.

I could ignore his request. I could let him lapse into sleep and hope he forgets to ask the next dragon. *I could spare him that knowledge.* But I owe him better than that. He should at least know there's hope for his brothers now.

"Well, as I told you before, I had every intention of killing her," I say, softly—maybe my voice will lull him to sleep. "My venom-tipped blade was ready. No more dragons would die because of a witch betraying us. I went after her, but I was too slow. She saw me coming. Well, she saw *us* coming —the mated dragons were faster with their fancy teleportation tricks."

A corner of Grigore's mouth twitches into a smile, so I know he's still awake.

"She's tall. Red-haired. Beautiful like you only see in a dream. I don't know if that's what made me hesitate. Maybe it was the look in her eyes…" Her eyes were dark brown and somehow wild in a way that caught my breath. The first encounter I had with her was sudden and strange and brutal—and landed me on the floor by some magic I still don't understand. But this second time… "I hesitated, and then she says, in this thick Irish accent, 'Ah, so it's you then.' And I just stood there like an idiot as she stepped forward, flipped up my visor, and placed her palm on my forehead." I pause and check Grigore's breathing. Low. Steady. I can't tell if he's asleep. I lower my voice even more, but I lean forward in my chair. "She showed me images—*in my mind*, Grigore—and they were of other women. Ones being held by the Vardigah." Those are the dark elves I thought the witch—Alice O'Rourke, according to Cinder—was working for. But I was wrong. "*Soul mates*, my brother. Dozens of them. And Alice was seeking my help to bring them home." I wait for a reaction from him, some sign that news of our literal salvation possibly being at hand had reached him… and nothing.

He just keeps sleeping—a sleep he may never wake from.

I let him rest.

Besides, I have another visit to make.

The hospice is on the ground floor of the dormitory that's a safehouse. It's separate from the North Lair, on a different island in the Thousand Islands from the home lair, partly to give everyone a space to retreat. A short elevator ride takes me up to the main floor of the dormitory, and a jaunt down the hall gets me to the room of one Julia McGovern. She's a twenty-five-year-old, dark-haired beauty, and a very popular woman given she's possibly a Dragon Spirit, the other half to a dragon somewhere in the world… assuming the Vardigah haven't destroyed the dragon part of her soul. There's no way to tell other than to go through the gauntlet—a True Kiss from each dragon until a match can be found. But given the Vardigah tortured and starved her, Niko has put a strict limit on how much romancing is allowed. Dragons rotate through, so she's kept company, but everyone has an interest in Julia's recovery, and no one's supposed to be actively seducing the poor woman.

There are still two dragons lined up outside her door and another inside.

I know my shift is next, so I tell Kass and Petr to beat it. Saryn is inside, but Julia seems to be ignoring him, reading a book on her kindle. He's a younger dragon, one of Renn and Ketu's second batch of children—mated dragons have waves of fertility, and they're one of the oldest pairs. Saryn's probably thirty now—real years not just appearance-wise—but he looks a little hapless on his plastic chair. I wave him off, and he seems grateful to retreat out the door. I follow him, close it, then drag the chair to Julia's bedside, turning it backward so I can straddle it.

"You the new babysitter?" she asks without lifting her gaze from her book.

"I've got a few questions for you."

She looks up, startled. "Constantine!" It's good she remembers me from the rescue.

I smile. "Hey. How are you doing?"

"Better, actually." She sets her kindle on the table beside her bed. "Sorry, I didn't realize it was you. It's just been..." Her vague wave at the door says it all. A constant stream of men, all hoping she's their soul mate, yet all forbidden from actually romancing her, so they spend their time figuring ways to cheat. And being strange about it all. Julia's been read in on everything—usually, that's a big deal, but the woman had already been captured by the Vardigah. Unlike Cinder, she remembered every minute. Explaining that dragon shifters had rescued her and that she might be the soul mate of one of them had little shock value.

"Sorry about that." And I mean it. I've romanced thousands of women over the years. Brought hundreds through the gauntlet. Most are thrilled at first. Heady with sexing it up with one partner after another. But I see the full cycle. I know the toll it takes. And that's for women who haven't been traumatized recently.

"It's okay." Her smile is forced. "I know it's important. I'm just, you know..."

"Still recovering? Because those bastard elves

tried to break you? I can imagine that might take more than a few days." It's been exactly three and a half since the raid. I'm counting the minutes. Alice-the-witch promised she'd help liberate the rest of the soul mates, but insisted we had to wait until she contacted us. Only I've been waiting my whole damn life, and I wasn't a patient dragon to begin with. "But you look great," I say with real enthusiasm. "Are you sleeping okay?" Word had it nightmares plagued her at first. But now there's a shine in her eyes, and her cheeks aren't so sunken as when we found her.

"Yeah, sleeping well." She tucks her long, dark hair back. "And I'm able to eat solid food again. I don't know who you have for a chef, but damn, the food's good. Or maybe I've just been starving for two weeks."

"It's actually that good." I smile, but that part hurts. *Two weeks.* And who knows how long the others have been tortured and starving. *And still are.* "Look, I know you don't know anything about the other soul mates, but I have some questions about Alice. If you're up for it."

"Sure." She folds up her legs and sits straighter.

"Do you know how she came to be working with the Vardigah?"

"No, sorry."

"Did she say anything about *how* she would get you and the others free?"

She shrugs. "Just that she was working on it. Honestly, most of the time I saw her, I was in pretty bad shape. She came in after the sessions. My mind was... scrambled. She'd do her magic thing, and that would help, but usually, I was zonked after."

I pull in a breath. "Is there anything you can tell me about her?" I'm desperate for any read on this.

She frowns, thinking. "She's kind of... intense? Or maybe just awkward? I mean, it was such a weird situation, right? But it seemed like there was something off about her."

That plays havoc with every nerve I have. "Like she's keeping a secret? Or lying about something?" This is my terrible fear. The thing keeping me up at night. *A witch* put her hand to my forehead and convinced me to go along with her plans. Aleks and Niko are still halfway convinced she put a hex on me. Only the hope of so many soul mates to be rescued keeps them open to this being real.

Julia's shaking her head. "No, nothing like that. She's great. Sweet but in an intense kind of way. That doesn't make much sense." She bites her lip, thinking harder.

"It's okay. Don't worry about it." I already understand the intensity part—I experienced that first hand.

Julia snaps her fingers then points one at me. "It's like she's a little… *feral.*" Then she puts up her hands as if to stop me from reacting, but it's too late —my heart lurches with that word. "That sounds bad," she hastily adds. "I mean she's like a wild kitten. You know how they're skittish when you first approach them, but they're really just hungry and scared? She was like that. Only powerful because she could do all this crazy magic. But I always had the sense that she was kind of… lost."

Now my chest is squeezing for an entirely different reason. "Like maybe she was a prisoner, too."

Julia's eyes go wide. "*Yes.* Exactly like that."

I rub a hand across my face, trying to wipe away a sudden torrent of emotion. In all my scouring of the world for dragon-spirited women, I've stumbled across plenty who've been held captive—*trafficked*— by men worse than beasts. These men do not fare well when I find them. The women—and often they are barely more than girls—I bring back to the safe-house. They have a refuge here in the dormitory, as long as they like. If the Vardigah are holding Alice against her will, forcing her to use her magic to destroy rather than heal… I can all too easily believe that story. But it could still be an illusion. She could be playing me for a fool, and all my brother dragons would pay the price.

Julia's peering at me. "You okay?"

I laugh a little. "I'm the one who's supposed to ask that question." I shake my head. "She said to wait for her. That she would tell me how to rescue the rest of the women. But it's been *three days*—how long am I supposed to wait?"

She shrugs. "Do you still have the mirror she gave you?"

I reach into my light jacket and pull it out. It's edged in gold carvings, and its black surface is as reflective as a true mirror. "I keep it with me constantly."

She nods. "That seems like a good plan."

I shake my head at my own reflection in the black glass. "I shouldn't be bothering you with this."

"It's better than wondering when the guy babysitting me is going to work up the nerve to kiss me."

I look up and grin. "That obvious, are they?"

But she's not laughing. "What about you?"

"Me?"

"Are you going to try to kiss me, too?" She's holding her breath.

I only hesitate a fraction of a second, all my instincts kicking in. "Do you want me to?"

"No, I was just wondering…" She flushes and drops her gaze. "This whole thing is weird."

"It is." I rise up from the plastic chair and ease onto the bed next to her.

"Oh, my God, please don't." She's waving me off like I might try to plant a kiss on her in her hospital bed.

"They're putting pressure on you." I keep my voice calm, but I'm already tallying up names of asses to kick.

"No, they're really not." She won't look at me.

"Then what's wrong?" I soften my voice even more.

"Nothing's wrong." Her arms are folded up now, capturing her legs. "I'm just embarrassed. What a stupid thing to say."

"What's *stupid* is this situation we've put you in." I dip my head to catch her gaze. "You are a beautiful dragon spirit who's been through hell and come out the other side."

She gives me a soft look. "Yeah. Except for that beautiful part. I'm no Cinder Dubois."

My eyebrows lift. "Are you serious?" The torture has taken its toll, but I've yet to meet a dragon spirit who wasn't beautiful and strong, inside and out.

"I mean, look at me." She holds out her arms, thin and pale, as if those should count as evidence against her.

"I am." I hold her gaze. "And I'm reconsidering that kiss."

She blinks and her lips part—she's holding her breath again. And while it goes against every edict Niko has laid down, I know when a woman is ready to be kissed... and when not being kissed will cause more damage than taking the risk.

I cup her cheek and run my thumb across her lower lip, then lean in and stop just before I reach her. "Every dragon wishes he were me right now." Then I press my lips to hers, swiping my tongue to part her lips, gently tasting. I feel her shudder in my hold. I take it deeper just for a moment, to put a little heat into something she's clearly thought about, maybe even hungered for. I'm the only dragon here she knows—the only one who *rescued her* who isn't already mated. I know the impact that can have. The instant connection it can forge.

I pull back before it goes on too long. She's affected, and it stabs me a bit... because that was a

True Kiss on her part, even if my heart is long-since dead. And since that heart wasn't just now magically brought back to life, one thing is certain. *Julia McGovern is not my soul mate.*

I stroke her hair back from her face. "I probably shouldn't have done that." But I can tell by the way her eyes are lit, all awkwardness and doubt banished—it was exactly the right thing to do. She needs to feel *alive* again. To have hope that something good can come of all this. It won't be with me, but she'll never open her heart to a long line of dragons if she doesn't start with the first one.

Her eyes are searching mine, worried. "Will you get in trouble?"

A small laugh erupts out of me. Then I give her a mischievous look. "I only did what every dragon in the lair is angling to do. Let them try to fault me for that."

"I don't know about *every* dragon." She drops her gaze to her hands. Does she really not see how beautiful she is?

I take her hand and give it a gentle squeeze. "You are literally *hope personified* to these dragons. No one wants to rush you, but you realize they're literally lined up out the door, right? There's only one that belongs with you—only one that's your other half. But every single one is hoping it's *them*. Take your time, but give them a chance. Give *both* of you the chance to find each other."

She looks at me with an unspoken question in her eyes.

So I answer it. "It's not me." Which I could have told her before the kiss. It's not impossible—my mate must be somewhere, her spirit still seeking mine. But I met her once, and lost her, two hundred years ago. It wouldn't take a True Kiss to recognize her again—I'm dead certain my heart would surge to life the moment we were in the same room.

But a True Kiss would seal it.

Julia seems a little disappointed... but not too much. I keep the smirk inside—the next dragon will have it much easier now. I need to tell Niko to lighten up on the restrictions.

Something buzzes behind me. On the bed —*what?*

I twist to see the mirror—the black mirror Alice gave me—shimmying on the white sheets.

"*Holy shit,*" Julia whispers. "Are you going to answer?"

Hell yes. I snatch it off the bed as I stand. Then I hold the mirror up, buzzing in my hands, with no clue what to do next. Suddenly, the vibration stops, and the blackness of the mirror fades…

Alice's rich brown eyes suddenly stare from the glass. "Can you talk?" she whispers, then throws a look over her shoulder. "Are you alone?"

"I… *yes*. Hold on."

Julia is already shooing me out of the room. I tuck the mirror into my jacket again and hurry out, quickly finding another room down the hall that's unoccupied. Then I pull the mirror back out— thank God she's still there. "I'm alone now." My heart's hammering.

Her fierce gaze captures me. "I need your help."

TWO

Alice

He's only a man—albeit a dragon-man—like the others.

Not that I've seen many men since I was a girl. But I don't know why *this* man's light brown eyes seem so much more alive than the others. Sure, he's a fine thing, but why does the beauty of his face seem so ancient and pure? His eyebrows are heavy, and he has this scruff of hair on his face that makes him rough. He keeps his hair long, like my cousin, my favorite, the one I remember was always going out to climb trees when he shouldn't. But *this* man, staring from my mirror portal with his scowl and his intensity, is no boy. Nor frivolous. Which is exactly why the fates sent him to me in a dream, I am sure, along with the twin soul mates, Cinder and her sister, Ember. This man's purpose is just as filled with destiny. I just didn't expect the flutter in my belly when those pale brown eyes are fixed on me.

"Do you have a plan?" he asks, adding, "To free the women."

As if there might be another plan afoot. "I'm working it." I glance behind me again, certain the Vardigah will return without my notice. Then back to the man with the eyes that make me flutter. "They're watching me all the time, now. Since you took Julia, they've lost their minds. More than normal that is."

There's a small smile, just a whisper of it, and the flutter kicks up. *Jesus, Mary, and Joseph.* "How can I help?" he offers.

My thoughts turn naughty with that. *What is wrong with you, Alice?* "I know little of your people, the dragons. Or your magic, although the impressive display of the other day caught my notice."

The small smile grows up into a beautiful thing. "That was Niko, the Lord of our Lair. Taking off one of the Vardigah's heads seems a fair payback for what they've done to Julia. And Cinder."

"Yeah, but I was speaking of the transport." Although the appearance of the dragon put the heart crossways in me, just for a moment.

"Teleportation," he corrects me.

"Whatever you call it, I need to know how it works."

But a frown gathers on his forehead, and he hesitates. And I haven't the bloody time for that. The elves could return at any moment to find me talking to my mirror.

"Have you got a name?" I ask quickly.

"Constantine." The whisper of a smile is back.

"All right, then, *Constantine…*" I like the sound of it, all rich and ancient. "There are twenty-six more of your dragon soul mates here in the elvish realm, and I don't have to tell you their state. Meanwhile, the Vardigah have doubled their guards, and I'm rarely left to myself. If we've any hope of hatching a plan to liberate these women, I need to know what you've got up your sleeve."

He frowns but says, "Only a few of us can teleport."

"How many?"

"Not enough for twenty-six rescues." He scowls. "And we need to know where they are."

"And how do you discern that?"

He presses his lips together.

My head is wrecked trying to drag this out of him. "Constantine, I am not your enemy. I would have thought I'd have earned your trust by now. Did I not send Ember to you?"

"What?" He frowns, but the suspicion wears away.

"Haven't you figured it out yet?" I glance behind me again. "I'm sure they'll come after me in a minute." I hold the mirror closer. "Come here to me, and I'll tell you. But then we've got to sort how to get your women free. I don't know how much longer they'll last. And I can't be protecting them all."

"I'm listening." And those eyes are still giving me the flutters.

"I knew, when I divined the dragon spirits in Ember and Cinder, that they were the key—"

"You used the Gift to find them."

"Yeah. Could you stop interrupting me for a second? Because we won't get there from here if you don't."

He blesses me with that smile again, the one full of beauty and heat. "Sorry."

"Right, then." I ignore the way that heat travels my whole body. "So I guided the Vardigah to Cinder, knowing Ember would come looking for her. Their dragon spirits are strong, and being twinned and *marked*, I knew if it were possible, she would find a way. They have an aura of destiny about them. But I knew Ember would need help. So I left that note in Cinder's calendar saying she was heading on to the party at Lord's castle. That way, Ember would find the dragons who could help her. Once Cinder was here in the Vardigah realm, I—"

"Wait," he says, interrupting me *again.* "You know where the lair is?" He looks like a snake has just slithered up his trousers.

"Well, *of course.* How do you think the Gift *works?*" Jaysus, if I have to explain *everything,* we've no hope at all.

"But you haven't told the Vardigah?" His discomfort eases, but I don't give a shite now.

"Would you be standing there, if I had?" I want to say, *Are you thick?,* but it seems impolite. And as little as I get to talk to humans—and usually they're women in need of healing, not men with eyes that make my insides flutter—I try to remember *some* manners. Even then, I think I get it all wrong, as it appears the case with Constantine and his confused but lovely face.

"No, I suppose not," he says. "But thanks all the same. I wasn't quite sure if we could trust you."

That wounds me. Like a dagger through my heart, and *what the hell, Alice?* How can I be soft on a man I barely know? Although, I suppose I know him better than any other. First, he grabbed me away from healing Cinder with those strong arms. And his face entranced me—I'd seen it in a dream, but somehow in the flesh, he was even more beautiful. When he came after me a second time, in my workshop, I stopped him with my words and a small protective hex to slow his intent. Just enough to get him to listen—and so I could use the memory spell to show him why I'd brought them all here in the first place. And now... he's just now deciding I'm not a threat to him and his people. It shouldn't bother me, but it does.

"You can trust me, Constantine," I say. "I'm not the one who brought a dagger to a rescue with murder on his mind."

He opens his mouth then thinks better of it, dropping his gaze. "I thought you were working with the Vardigah."

"You're not wrong about that."

He looks up sharply like I've poked him with a stick.

"It's a bit more complicated. I'll explain it all when we have time to drink tea by a fire. In the meantime, things are rather pressing, what with all the torture happening. But I swear on my mother's ashen grave, I will give every last measure to free these women. With your help. Do I have it?"

He frowns, but nods.

"How many dragons can you bring when you transport?" I ask. "I see you linking hands and arms. How far does the magic reach?"

"Up to four people at a time. Approximately. Depending on the size." He grimaces like this isn't information he parts with easily. "But like I said, only some of us can do it."

"All right. We'll have to figure the numbers on that, but the dragon spirits are each held in a separate cell, and you'll have to gather them all at once. The Vardigah are hoping to capture one of you and use your minds against you—to discover where you are in the human realm. We can't let that happen."

"Agreed." He's paying full attention now.

"The Vardigah have to know a place to transport to it—they need some sense of its location. Which is why they cannot know yours. Are dragons the same? I've seen you appear in places you couldn't possibly have known. Or is your teleportation like my Gift, where I sense a person's essence and divine their place from that?"

"We're a little of both—we could find the Vardigah realm or teleport somewhere on Earth, but to find Julia, we had to have someone who had a connection to her."

I frown. "Assuming we can sort that, you *will* need at least twenty-six dragons who can transport, eh, teleport—one for each dragon spirit in a simultaneous strike. And we'll need more dragons for support, three if you can manage it, in case things go arseways. We'll figure out the rest—" A noise behind me kicks my heart. I quickly wave my hand across the mirror and mumble the spell. *Terminus.* Then I hastily set it down on the workbench and turn.

Jarod stands at the far end of my workshop. Elvish expressions are always subtle, but I've been among them longer than my own people, so I can tell. His suspicion lives in the twitch of his long ears, extending well above his head, and I can see that even at this distance.

"Practicing your arts?" he calls in Elvish. The Vardigah stubbornly refuse to learn human languages. I had to acquire theirs, mainly from Jarod, my "master" since I was brought here. I also learned a bit from one of the ancient spellbooks of my mother's. I have no idea how a complicated spell in Elvish got into a book of ancient Irish witchings, but there it was. Never mind it was a

death hex. That should have been my first warning, but I was just a child.

"One can't be too careful around one's enemies," I reply in his elvish tongue.

In a blink, he transports closer. The now-black mirror on my bench draws his gaze. *"What sorcery is this?"*

Mirrors are for scrying, portals, and the like. They can even reflect a spell, as a defensive art, but I haven't mastered that. Thankfully, I discovered the lies of the Vardigah before I'd fully come into my magic, so most of my craft has remained hidden from the prying eyes of Jarod and the other Vardigah he brings to my workshop, showing off his pet witch.

It's easy to lie to them—the challenge is keeping the lies right in my head.

"Enhancement," I say. *"If the dragons return, I will need stronger arts to defend myself."*

"Prudent." A high compliment from Jarod. I relax a tiny amount. *"I've brought you nourishment. Do you require more supplies for your arts?"*

"What I have suffices." But I peer at the boxes piled at the far end. The elves subsist entirely on a syrup that's grown somewhere in their realm. I tried it when I first arrived because I was literally starving

—and the syrup nearly struck me dead. Since then, the elves have periodically raided the human world and brought me things they thought were food. Any cooking was up to me, which meant I was dying to crack open my mother's spellbooks and learn to conjure fire. I almost burned down my workshop—my bed, books, witching supplies, everything—which would have been tragic, given it holds all I have left of my home. My true home, in the human realm, not this tiny, dank corner of the elvish one.

I give Jarod a nod and head on to the new food supplies, but he grabs my arm. I pull out of his grasp but stay by him, automatically obedient. Weeks without food and the occasional caging in small boxes taught me early to obey without thinking. Survive first; ponder the horrors of it later.

"The feast can wait." He curls a lip. Elves find my human habits, like eating, quite disgusting. *"You are needed in cell twenty-two."*

I can't travel myself—that's not a power that witches possess—which means Jarod is here to collect me for more "duties." My consent is not required, but I stand straight, hands at my side, to signal I'm ready. Unlike the dragons, the Vardigah do not need to lock hands to bring you along. As long as you're close, they possess the power to drag you off through interdimensional space until you've arrived where you're going. Which could be bloody anywhere, but as I told Constantine, the Vardigah must know the *place* to which they are going. This is why they need me to guide them to the dragon spirits—and why Jarod brings me in a blink to cell twenty-two, not specifically to the human named Lily who is pinned in a restraint chair.

I know this cell, as I do all the others. They remind me I carry the burden of their torture every time I see the wreckage of it. Cell twenty-two contains the restraint chair, two Vardigah technicians, and Lily. Sometimes, the captured women are taken out of their cells. I'm not sure where the Vardigah go with them—I think for some display or report to the rest of the elvish community—but most of the torture takes place here.

Lily is shaking even though they've finished the session. I stride over and go about my business, placing my hand on her forehead. The two technicians back up to allow me room. I close my eyes to give a show of focusing on my dark art. Supposedly, I'm searching for the ragged remnants of Lily's dragon spirit—the thing the Vardigah are trying to destroy. In reality, I could find her spirit anywhere across the two realms, both Vardigah and human.

It's the Gift of my people—we carry it in our blood. Our brilliant and beautiful craft was once used for good, if my mother's books are to be believed. As the story goes, witches had a strong alliance with the dragon folk, each helping the other. The witches found their mates; the dragons donated their blood, spit, and even their magic-rich bones after death for the witching arts.

Now, the Vardigah force me to use my Gift on these women. To capture them. To break them. Which brings me a good deal of shame every day.

So I keep my abilities as secret as possible. I tell the Vardigah I must travel to Earth to find new dragon mates. I say the dragons themselves are invisible to me. And I, with no small amount of drama, place my hand on Lily's smooth, light-brown forehead to sense any remnants of her dragon spirit. In reality, I'm filling her with healing magic to counter the damage they've done.

I can't decide if the Vardigah are thick shites or if their disdain for the human realm—especially dragons and witches—blinds them. As if I'm too stupid to fool them. They are a very literal people, but I'm an orphaned witch who barely taught herself the craft. They have ridiculous powers and boundless magic. I shouldn't be able to—

Lily stirs under my hand.

"This will take some time," I tell the nearest technician in Elvish. I want them to leave so I can reassure her with words and not just magic.

"We will stay," Jarod commands, both to the technicians and me.

I sigh and redouble my efforts. They won't let me linger long before requiring an answer. And my choice is a bitter one. Either I say her dragon spirit remains, thus ensuring more torture, or I say it's been shattered, in which case, I'm certain her fate would be worse. I'd like to think they'd return her to the human realm and let her live her remaining days, but I'm not an idiot. I lied about the one woman whose dragon spirit they've managed to destroy. They continued to torture her. I pray that was the right choice.

In the end, it's no choice at all.

I step back from Lily, my healing magic depleted anyway. Her skin is less gray, her cheeks less sunken, but she doesn't awake. It's just as well.

"She remains dragon spirited." I turn to Jarod. *"But her body is weak. She should rest."* They fear killing the women outright—they'd have to start over as the dragon spirits are set free, seeking new baby girls to be born into. I know it happens within a day. I

know the Vardigah wouldn't hesitate to hunt down that newly born child and torture it. So I lie about that too, saying it could take years to re-manifest. That a dead woman is a lost spirit, at least temporarily.

They believe me.

And that's the only thing I have going for me.

THREE

Constantine

"*Twenty-six?*" Niko rubs his hand along the back of his neck. "You sure?"

"As sure as I can be." We're in his office. I came straight here after Alice's connection got cut, which still has my stomach in knots. I know the dragon spirits are the ones I should be worried about, but if the Vardigah caught her talking to a dragon, the very people they're trying to wipe out—

"And you're sure we can't do this in shifts?" Niko asks.

"The whole thing is a huge risk," I say. "I get that. But how can we *not* go, Niko? Think of it— twenty-six new soul mates. Over two dozen newly mated pairs? It would save us. Finally. For real—no more talk of extinction. We'd finally have a chance—"

He holds up a hand to stop me. "If it's not a massive trap to finish us off for good."

"Alice wouldn't do that," I protest.

"*Alice.*" Niko gives me a pinched look I don't care for. "She's a witch, Constantine. Aleks is convinced she put a hex on you."

I wince. Because I'm not sure he's wrong. "You don't have to trust my judgment on this. She knows where the lair is."

"*Fuck.* That's just great." He pushes off the desk he was perched on and runs his hands through his hair. "Do we need to move?" The panic is ramping up on his face. He starts to pace.

"That's just it—she's known all along."

Niko stops short and pivots back. "What? Are you sure?"

"Positive. And if she was going to betray us, the lair would already be burned to the ground." Although, I'd be convinced even without that compelling little factoid. Alice and I didn't talk long, but it was enough—I could see the spitfire in her eyes that Julia mentioned. Alice is a fierce kitten, all teeth and claws and sarcasm, but her heart shines through every word. And given that she's so young and beautiful, and the Vardigah have her under lock and key—the itching need to rescue *her* is just as strong as bringing the dragon spirits out of their hellholes.

Niko's back at the desk, leaning against it and frowning. "Okay, let's assume she's telling the truth. Twenty-six simultaneous rescues from the Vardigah realm? Any clue how we're going to do that?"

I grimace because there are all kinds of problems with this. "It'll take nearly every mated dragon on the planet."

"Nearly every *dragon,*" Niko insists. "She wants three unmated dragons as a backup brigade for every mated one? And twenty-six of those? That's over a hundred total dragons, more than double our forty here in the North Lair."

"Forty-two, now with Ember and Cinder," I offer.

"Forty-one." Niko's scowl is dark. "We lost Yiannis. And Grigore won't be with us long."

Fuck. "Right." I pull in a breath. "So we go to the Euro Lair. And the South Asian Lair is growing, I hear. What about the Beijing Lair? Any word from them?"

"They're still scattered. I'm not sure what

happened there, but we can't count on them for now."

"Okay." I counted it up on my way over. "We've got sixteen mated dragons here, including you and Aleks and your new mates. Last I heard, the Euro Lair has four, and South Asia has eight. That's a total of twenty-eight, so if we recruit *everyone* to this, we can rescue all the women. What's the headcount on unmated dragons?" Those are harder to track, given babies are being born as often as the mated pairs can manage. They grow up so fast, by the time I turn around, they're out scouting for mates.

"Shit, I don't know." He reaches back and grabs a pad of paper off his desk. "You're making me do fucking math?"

I smirk. "Sorry."

"All right," Niko says, scribbling. "Euro Lair just has a few kids, and nobody like Grigore, so I'm guessing nineteen there. South Asian Lair has a bunch of kids, so…" He taps the pencil against his lips, whispering. "Okay, that's seven kids and seventeen full-grown dragons. We're looking at…" More scribbling. "Fuck—not enough. Okay, if we don't have a full complement of three with every mated dragon…" He scratches some more on the paper and swears again. Then he sucks in a breath.

"Looks like we only have enough for two unmated dragons per mated dragon on the mission. With a couple extra. That's assuming my numbers are current and we can actually get every fucking dragon on the planet over the age of eighteen to storm the Vardigah realm." He tosses the pad back on his desk. "What the hell are we doing here? Risking the entire species? Leaving behind kids to fend for themselves?"

"I'll admit that seems… risky." My stomach is hard as a rock.

"Damn right, it's risky." He sighs then gives me a pointed look. *"You* are talking the other lairs into this, not me."

I shrug one shoulder. "Can you at least give me a lift?" Teleportation is the only way to do this.

He scowls. "We need to get our own lair on board first. Including *all* the mated dragons. Which means little orphaned dragons if this goes sideways. We'll have to leave a few unmated dragons behind to take care of the kids."

"Maybe we just send the mated dragons with no backup?" I offer. That seems like a terrible idea.

Niko shakes his head like the whole thing is nuts. Which it is. "No, the witch is right. The more dragons we send, the more likely we are to get the mated ones—and the new soul mates—back home in one piece. There were like *five* of us going after Julia, and that was sketchy as hell."

"Maybe we can break the attack into two waves."

"That would be *so* much easier."

I frown because I'm sure Alice is *not* going to like that plan. And she's right—the Vardigah will lose their fucking minds if we show up *en masse*. "They might just start killing the soul mates."

"Fuck." Niko runs both hands into his hair again.

Now that I think about it, I'm almost certain that will happen. "Maybe if we're fast, we can make it work. Hopefully, I can work with Alice on that." Except that magic mirror of hers only dials one way —and I have no idea what's happening on her end.

What a fucking disaster.

"Okay, you do that." Niko boosts up from the desk. "I'll talk to the mated dragons. You gather up the unmated ones. Tell them what we're facing. Tell them Ember and I are in—I'm sure she'll want to go back for the others—but not everyone can go. We need dragons to stay behind for the kids. Got it?"

"Yeah."

"We'll need our own lair solid on this before we try to get the others on board."

I nod, and Niko disappears, teleporting out of the office to who knows where. He and Ember are still honeymooning at his retreat. Aleks and Cinder are full-time at the cottage. We'll be risking all the dragons capable of continuing the species on the chance of bringing back mates for the rest of us—and not even everyone. *Twenty-six.* It's a miraculous number given we've found six soul mates for our lair and a few for the others over two centuries. Ember and Cinder don't count—that was Alice's doing, sending them here precisely to get our help in rescuing the others. And somehow I have to sell that story to the unmated dragons—they will be as skeptical as Niko.

I wish they could see Alice for themselves. Her fiery attitude. Her determination to save the women from the Vardigah. The entire lair has been on fire since word spread that there were potentially so many mates captured by our mortal enemies. The excitement has revved everyone up. Maybe that will carry the day. But hearing it straight from Alice would help.

I pull out my phone and text the group chat—the one reserved for emergency meetings lair-wide.

That should bring every dragon in the house into the main hall. A couple are down in the city, scouting—I'll call them after, but I send a text for them to head home now. I don't know how fast we can pull all this together, but we need all hands on deck.

It takes some time, but a half-hour later, I've got everyone murmuring and shifting from foot-to-foot in the main hall. I count sixteen dragons—Pollux and Akkan have already texted that they're on their way from the city. Eighteen doesn't seem like a lot when their uneasy energy rattles in the hall, and it's even fewer to carry the fate of the species on their backs. But we've all been doing that for two centuries. Now they finally have a real chance at a mate, not the million-to-one odds that come in romancing endless numbers of the general public, no matter how well I screen the women I recruit.

I'm hardly one for speeches, but that's probably the best approach. "You've all heard about the soul mates the Vardigah have captured," I start, and everyone settles down. "Most of you have met the one we brought back. You saw what shape she was in. How they tortured and starved her. Well, there are *twenty-six* more like her, and each one is a soul mate for some dragon. Maybe you. Maybe the next dragon. But that's a hell of a lot of women the Vardigah are tormenting because they are our other halves—our dragon spirits. They belong *here*, with us." A strong murmur of approval goes up with that. "Or at least out of the clutches of the fucking elves." Several *hell yeses* echo through the hall. "Here's how this goes: we're coordinating a massive, simultaneous assault. It will require virtually every dragon—mated and unmated—on the planet. A few will have to stay behind with the children— Renn and Ketu's kids, Adara and Vasil's baby, Shujin and Rhox's little one. That's critical—you know the mated dragons are taking a tremendous risk to bring our soul mates home. They need to know their families are safe. But beyond that, we're going to need every able-bodied dragon ready to suit up and risk their necks to make this operation happen. Think about it. Come see me with your questions. But we're going to be deciding this soon."

"I don't need to think about it," says Kashin, his arms folded, feet planted, standing at the front of the group. "I'm ready to go now."

I smile. "Understood."

"Me, too." Stephanos is even stronger in his pledge.

A chorus rises up, sudden and sharp, everyone

insisting that they're all-in and that we should leave immediately.

"All right, my brothers." I raise my hands in surrender. "I hear you. You'll need to decide amongst yourselves who stays behind. I'll let Niko know the North Lair is ready for this mission." They give a collective shout—exuberance and determination—and I dismiss them with a smile and a shake of my head, but my heart is full. There was no question, no hesitation. Not even the worry that somehow, I'm under the hex of a beautiful witch. They trust me—really, their faith is in Niko, as it should be.

I wave Stephanos over as the others cluster into groups. "We're going to need fireproof suits," I tell him. "A lot of them. Can you handle it, my brother?"

"Of course," he says. "I'll check with Aleks on specs and get it done." He hustles off to make it happen.

The others mill around, arguing with each other about who should stay and who should go. Getting the other lairs on board won't be this easy, but at least we have this. Assuming Alice wasn't found out by her Vardigah captors. Which reminds me how little I know about the witch we're all following into battle—and how intensely I *want* to know. What's her story? How does a young witch, fully capable in her craft, get swept up by the Vardigah? Her ancestors were supposedly all wiped out—but then again, so were ours. Except dragons live a long damn time —some days, I feel all two hundred and twenty-five years. Witches may extend a few dozen more years with healing or rejuvenation spells—or borrowed dragon blood—but they're mostly human. And Alice is *young*—I'm guessing no more than twenty. She was born in this time, not a survivor from a bygone era. How? And are there more like her? I tell myself my worry for her fate and my intense desire to know her story are in service to my people —for my dragon brothers and their mates.

But the truth is I'm fascinated by *her.*

I've romanced uncountable women, and it's been a long damn time since one captured my attention so thoroughly. Is it because she's the one woman in the world I have no reason to seduce? Or is it the feral kitten way she hisses at me and puts me in my place? She's obviously beautiful and painfully smart, in a savvy kind of way, a sharpness that has always been my weakness in a woman. And that mouth… more than once, while she was flaying me with her wit, I imagined the taste of it. Of her.

And that's a ridiculous thing to do in the midst of a desperate mission to save lives. And hearts.

Maybe, once is this through… I know Alice needs rescuing as much as the others. I need to remind Niko of that since the accounting on this will be so tight. But if I survive the rescue, I'm going to find out if Alice's lips are as sweet as they look—

"Fuck, *no!*"

My head jerks up. A crowd has converged on someone on the floor. *What the fuck?* I hurry forward, edging past the dragons doing the same, trying to see.

"Kashin," someone sobs.

"Oh, *fuck."* The murmurs grow louder. Some-one's down.

By the time I reach the center, someone says, "It's just like Yiannis. *Shit."*

Kashin's lying on the floor, eyes wide open, staring at the ceiling as if he slipped and fell and simply stayed down, stunned. Only he's not moving, and the surprise on his face is horribly familiar. We only buried Yiannis a few days ago.

Everyone is stunned. One of the younger dragons is openly sobbing over Kashin's body. I'm as speechless as anyone. I stumble back. The eyes of every dragon follow me.

All except Kashin.

"I'll… go tell Niko," I mumble. Then I turn and stride for the stairs, the hot breath of destiny on the back of my neck.

We're running out of time.

FOUR

Alice
_____

No, no, no.

Healing magic pumps through my palm and into the forehead of the blonde-haired woman seated before me, but it's like pouring water into a bucket made of holes. Sarah's pale face has gone ghostly white, and I can find no trace of the dragon spirit there just a day ago. Or was it two? I'm not privy to the Vardigah's torture schedule—they bring me in when they need me. My bumbling magic is nothing against the destructive power of their psychic wand. Sarah's nearly as still as death already—her breathing is shallow, and her mind is a field of wreckage.

"Does her dragon spirit yet remain?" Jarod demands of me in Elvish.

It's gone, but there's no more avoiding the question. I've been desperately pushing healing magic in her for going on ten minutes now, but I can't resurrect what's lost. I know Jarod—someone else will pay for his failure to destroy the dragon spirits. He will gleefully kill Sarah, and the next, and the next after that, to make it happen. I can't decide if it's more dangerous or less to give this victory to him.

But Sarah won't survive another round in the torture chair.

I lean back and announce, *"Her dragon spirit is gone."*

Jarod strides over with uncharacteristic speed. *"You are certain?"* He looms over her chair, peering at her face as if he could see the absence of it there.

"Yes." *Jaysus,* I hope this is the right choice.

"Ah! Finally." Jarod makes a fist and swirls it in the air. I have no idea the meaning of that, but the technicians start bowing in some elaborate display of fealty.

I step closer to Sarah and put my hand on her shoulder. *"Let me take her back to my living space,"* I say, attempting to forestall whatever plan he had.

"For what purpose?" His ears twitch with suspicion.

I hunt for an excuse. *"She can assist me in my arts."*

He snorts, a sign that's not quite agreement but also not argument. To the technicians, he says, *"Revive her."*

I want to stop them—it's better if I care for her myself—but they shove me aside to place a wand to her head. She jerks and twitches and then… falls absolutely still. The chair which binds her squeals an alarm. I step further back, tears crowding my eyes, as the technicians fluster and try to jolt her back to life with their magic.

"Leave it!" Jarod snaps, and they hastily retreat. He turns to me. *"Maybe the next one will be stronger."*

I nod, dully, eyes down, so Jarod won't see the tears brimming. He says nothing more, just transports me to my workshop and then immediately transports away. Off to crow about his great success to the others.

I stand in front of my workbench, fighting the tears. I can't cry because there are twenty-six women who need me. *Twenty-five.* I wipe my eyes and shuffle forward. The bottles and supplies that were destroyed when Constantine and his dragon men came for Julia have been replaced. I pull a pot from the stores underneath and slowly, mechanically, gather the ingredients for a healing potion, like I have a hundred times before. *Wormwood.*

Butterfly wing. Blisterwort. Half a warbler's egg. I gather each from their jars and boxes, then grind them with a mortar and pestle of iron-laced granite, then into the pot they go. Next is a touch of the elvish syrup and a tincture of herbs I'd previously cooked, plus a large swig of human wine to make it go down. I set the pot on its stand and conjure a small blue flame to heat and congeal the magic in the ingredients. The ancient words come automatically to my tongue as I stir.

I tell myself Sarah's death isn't my doing. But it's a lie.

And the tears force their way out, regardless.

What of the rest of the women? Even if the dragons muster enough travelers to rescue every soul mate, and before Jarod kills them, how will the dragons find them? I'm the only one who knows each face, each name, each dragon spirit within. Which only reminds me—the death of Sarah's spirit means a dragon died today as well.

My heart is so heavy, it despairs that anything can be done. All my efforts count for nothing. *Worse* than nothing. Had I realized the Vardigah's plans sooner, I could have refused them. I would have paid a price—the greatest sin is to be useless to them, and my end will be coming soon enough anyway—but better that than all this blood on my hands.

The pungent smell of the healing potion fills my workshop. I take it from the heat and stir it to cool. I know dozens of potions, everything from a balm for a weak stomach to a nightshade poison that will bring death in minutes. Which I will use at some point. If I'm dead, the Vardigah can no longer use my magic for their evil ways. No more women would be brought to their realm. No more torture of their minds and spirits until I say *stop*. What right have I to go on, given what I've done? The question haunts me. It's only the desperate hope of my care-fully-hatched rescue plan that keeps me from cooking up a stew of death for supper.

The potion is ready. I pour it from the pot into a chalice and steel myself for the drinking. Its magic is only half in the ingredients—the other half comes from liberating life essence from my body, mobi-lizing it to be dispensed through my hands when the time comes. But the potion must exact its price from me first. This feels like punishment on a normal day, so today, I especially welcome it.

I knock the whole slurried mess back straight.

It makes me cough and sputter, but it stays down. I wipe my mouth and rinse the chalice, but

I'm no sooner done with that bit of housekeeping than my stomach cramps. The extraction has begun. I clutch my middle and head on to my cot in the corner. I breathe through the pain and stumble into the narrow bed. I'd like not to puke, so I allow myself a whimper or two to release the pain. Then I gather the blanket and notice the portal mirror tangled in it. I'd nearly called Constantine before, just so he'd know I was fine, but Jarod interrupted with his demands. Now that he's had his triumph, perhaps he'll leave me alone for a stretch.

I start to conjure the words to open the portal, then stop. I'm a mess, squirming in pain. And I've got no real plan for a rescue. I want Constantine to know I tried for Sarah, I truly did—and that I want to end all this—but I've no business calling the dragon man merely to see his face and gain his sympathy.

I clear the spell and keep the portal shut.

Steady on, Alice, I tell myself. *You've been through worse, girl.* Although it feels like a cataclysm this time. It's one thing to starve away in a box for daring to refuse Jarod's order, and it's another thing entirely to watch a woman die because of what you said. Or didn't say. I can't figure how I could have saved her, though. And her mate, somewhere in the human realm, who just met his demise. The cramping in my gut reminds me how human I am, despite the witching powers I've cobbled from the books of my people. I'm just one girl—barely a woman now. How can I be expected to stop the murder of an entire people? I can barely care for myself. I'm itching to open a portal to this dragon man, Constantine, but for what? Only to tell him my sorry state? As if he's a friend, not a random co-conspirator. I do remember having friends you could turn to. If not a friend, then an aunt or a cousin or a sister. In my tiny village, everyone knew you and your business. Everyone was someone you could trust to help, if they could keep their nose out of your business long enough. I've been alone for such a time, I've nearly forgotten what a friend does. They lend a hand. Or a shoulder to cry on. I should have a good cry *before* calling Constantine, but instead, I whisper the words to open the portal.

His beautiful face shows on the mirror, startled then relieved. *"Alice!* You're all right."

Not remotely true, but it feels good to hear him say it with such joy. "Ah, I could be worse." I'm propped on my side, looming over the portal. Probably not the most attractive view. "Hang on." I work my way to sitting, knees up, and balance the mirror there. My stomach cramps a bit in this position, but I manage it.

"I was afraid they'd found you out." He peers closer at me. "You okay?"

Do the tears show? Is my hair a state? It's a long, red mess on a normal day. I try to tame it by tucking it behind my ears. "I'm fine. Just checking on you and your dragons. I have a bit of bad news." I grimace because my stomach is having fits and I'm about to tell the man a soul mate has died and some dragon in the world has as well. Poor Sarah won't be the last if we don't hurry.

"So do I." He looks off-screen for a moment. "It's Alice," he says to whoever is in the room. "She's all right."

I squirm a little. Somehow, I'd thought this was a private chat. "Who's there?" I ask.

"Just Niko and some of the mated dragons. Hang on." Then he's on the move. I get to watch his lovely pale brown eyes looking ahead as we travel to somewhere. He closes a door, then looks directly in the mirror again. "Okay, we're alone now. What's going on? Did they hurt you? Because I'm looking for a reason to spill some Vardigah blood and that would work for me."

I blink. Too much. And I'm startled out of

words for a moment. "No, they didn't… I mean, they don't know I'm helping you." My whole face flushes hot. "Would you really come after them because of me?" This feels… *important.* I can't quite catch a breath.

He's scanning my face. "What have they done to you, Alice?" It's soft. Concerned. With a touch of deadly intent for the Vardigah underneath.

It flushes heat through my entire body. "I'll tell you the story of it, someday."

"I'd like to hear it." It's rough and… *sexual.*

Jaysus, the voice this man has. I'm losing all sense of what we're talking about.

"What's your bad news?" he prods gently.

My stomach twists with guilt about feeling heated when a woman and her mate just lost their lives. And because of me. "One of the soul mates— her name was Sarah—she passed. Her body just gave out. But before that, the Vardigah destroyed her dragon spirit. Which means somewhere in the world, there's a dragon who's likewise passed. I'm so sorry, Constantine. I did what I could to heal her. To protect her." And that much *is* true, even if I brought her to the Vardigah in the first place.

Constantine sighs and briefly closes his eyes. "I know. We lost our brother Kashin today."

"Oh, no." Somehow, I wasn't expecting it would be one of his friends. The tears surge back. "I didn't know… I'm so sorry… I couldn't stop them…" The tightness in my stomach is working up to my chest. I clutch the mirror so tight, it bites my palms. I look away.

"You did what you could," he says softly. "You can't blame yourself—"

"Can't I?" I wipe the self-pitying tears and glare through the mirror. "All my ancestors, my mother before me and her mother before her, we were healers. Matchmakers of dragons. We built families and tended hearts and souls and bodies. And here I am… the *destroyer* of lives." The shame of it burns. I've never said this out loud—who would I tell? Jarod? The women he tortures?

There's only sweetness in Constantine's eyes. "They're forcing you. None of this is your fault."

I don't want the excuses. And a deep, tremulous part of me fears his kindness is mercenary. He needs his mate—all his dragon brothers do. He needs my help. He would say anything, make any excuse, for me and my actions. It's not that witches and dragons cannot be friends—it's that a witch who has endangered them all doesn't deserve one.

I sniff back the tears. "We need to move quickly, Constantine. Others will fall soon."

He matches my serious tone. "How much time do we have?"

"I don't know." But the tightness in my chest eases. *Focus on saving those left, Alice.* "Sarah's not the first dragon spirit to fall, but she's the first the Vardigah know about. Now that they have that…" *Thanks to me,* the bitter voice in my head adds. "…they'll double their efforts to break everyone else. Tell me you've collected enough dragons for a rescue."

"Not yet." At my distress, he quickly adds, "Soon, though. I have to speak to the other lairs. But it will take convincing nearly every dragon on the planet. And we still won't have enough, not really. It would be better if we could do this in two waves."

"That won't work." I bite my lip in frustration. "The Vardigah would rather kill them than lose them, especially to you. You have to know that. Are there really so few of you?" I can sense them all, if I search, but I've purposely avoided it, to keep the dark elves from finding them.

"I'm afraid so," Constantine says. "And convincing everyone to risk everything won't be easy. They haven't seen what I've seen. They haven't met *you*."

"Why would meeting me make any difference at all?" That makes no sense.

"Because we haven't seen a witch in two hundred years," he says softly. "You have no idea what it means to my people just knowing you exist."

"Really?" I'm confused, but then it clicks, and hope bursts to life inside me. "Because of the Gift."

"We're dying as a people, Alice." His solemn, beautiful eyes hold me through the portal. "You have to know *that*."

"Because you haven't had a witch to pair you in two hundred years." This somehow escaped me before. My family were in hiding—they thought the dragons were dead. Of course, the dragons would think the same.

"These women are our salvation," Constantine says. "If I can just convince everyone that they're *real*—that *you're* real—then I know they'll risk anything to bring them home."

And I suddenly know how to accomplish it. "Come and get me, Constantine."

"What?" His eyebrows lift.

I lean closer to the mirror. "Do you remember when I put my palm to your forehead? And conjured the images of the women in your mind?" It was a tiny memory spell, transferring mine to his.

"Yes, but that's not enough for me to find them in the Vardigah realm," he protests. "And even if it were—even if I could guide a mated dragon who can teleport—I could only rescue one at a time."

"Which is why *I* need to come to *you.*" I sit up straighter because this plan could actually work. "My mother's books told the story of it. In times past, witches would place their hand upon a dragon's head and immediately sense their other half, no matter where in the world their soul mate might be. We were the conduit which made that first connection, but once it was made, the dragon could find his dragon spirit wherever she was."

Constantine's beautiful eyes have gone wide and filled with hope. "If they know where their mates are… there's no force on earth which could hold them back."

"Bring me to your dragons. That's all I need." And my heart lifts. *This is good.* Something *truly* good that I can do, and maybe, just maybe, it will redeem all the rest.

"I'll need a little time to prepare."

"Hurry." I have to prepare, as well. Pairing twenty-five dragons to their mates will take stamina.

I have a couple potions for that. "We should meet somewhere away from your lairs, though, just in case."

He nods quickly. "But how will I let you know when we're ready?"

"I'll check in whenever I can." I grimace. "And I can't be gone too long. They'll notice." If Jarod came and found me missing... it would not go well for any of us.

"Be careful, Alice. You're the key to all of this." He says it with such sweet concern, I can almost believe he means it like a friend—not merely because I'm the witch he needs to save his people.

"I'll see you soon." I whisper the words to close the portal. Constantine's coming to bring me to the human realm.

My steps out to my workshop have never been so light.

FIVE

Constantine

"How do you know she's truly a witch?"
Rajesh asks.

He's one of the mated dragons in the South
Asian Lair. It's the same question they asked at the
European Lair just an hour ago.

"I've seen Alice conjure a magic shield and cast
a memory spell," I say. "Not to mention the
Vardigah have been using her precisely because she
has the Gift." I've already said this, and I feel like
we're going in circles. Niko dropped me here then
quickly teleported away, leaving me to persuade the
eight mated and seventeen unmated adult dragons
of the South Asian Lair to join our rescue mission.
Leaving was a good choice—Niko needs to help
ferry the unmated dragons of both the North and

Euro Lairs to the meeting spot in Ireland, but I'm floundering here on my own. Thoughts of Alice— why she looked so distraught and what the Vardigah have done to her—keep distracting me.

"A memory spell?" Rajesh's skepticism is shared by the others gathered to hear the North Lair's fantastical story and dangerous proposal. "Have you considered she might have put a hex on you? That would explain all of this." Rajesh has the same dark hair, deep brown eyes, and Indian features of most dragons here. Although, his mate, Elizabeth, standing at his side and carrying their smallest child, little Sasha, is a soul mate we found in the Northern Lair. She's originally from Canada but circulated through the lairs until she found her mate. Their three sons have her brilliant blue eyes. That pairing fifty years ago was one of the things that bound the lairs together.

I sigh. "You're welcome to visit our lair. Talk to the women we've already rescued."

"They could have been under her spell as well," Elizabeth says, just as skeptical as her mate.

"The memory spell was *on me,*" I say, exasperated and knowing that doesn't help my case. "She showed me the women who had been captured. Trust me, this situation is real." To be fair, Aleks is also convinced Alice put me under a spell—and they're not wrong. It's just that it's the spell a woman like her has always cast on me. Strong women with whip-smart mouths. Tough on the outside and vulnerable, sweet, and broken on the inside. There's a reason most of the trafficking victims we've given refuge at the lair are ones I've brought in. I have a sense when something's off— when a woman is hiding something in the myriad ways they do. Pretending everything's fine. Acting tough to cover the shattered interior. Using their brilliant determination on the outside to hold everything together on the inside. At first, I thought Alice was a witch who had betrayed dragonkind because I sensed, right away, she was carrying dark and heavy secrets. I felt it from that first moment I held her to my chest, hauling her away from Cinder during the rescue. I should have known the beautiful red-haired woman in my arms was far more complicated than just a witch gone bad.

Women like her have always held me captive. I don't always want to take them to bed, but I *always* want to rescue them. With Alice, it's becoming painfully obvious that I most definitely want to do *both*. Which is inappropriate on almost any level, and yet the thought of her—learning her secrets, *being* with her—has completely taken over my mind.

Which means I'm distracted and missing Rajesh's diatribe about the follies of the Northern Lair. "...it's not as if we haven't looked for witches ourselves," he's saying. "You in the North spend your time sifting through thousands of women hoping to find one shining diamond of a soul mate. And we are grateful for that." He gives a small nod to his mate. "But *here*, we spend our time looking for the diamond-hunter. Witches are not unknown on the subcontinent, but we have yet to find any with the true Gift."

"That's what I'm *saying*, Rajesh. She's the real deal." I gesture to the crowd around us. The South Asian Lair is younger on average—they have seven still-small children between their four couples, compared to only six kids at the North Lair between the six couples. But our baby boom is coming, with Niko and Aleks and their mates. And that will be nothing compared to what happens if we rescue all the soul mates the Vardigah have captured. "If Alice is truly a witch, and what she's shown me is actually real—that there are *twenty-five* soul mates in desperate need of rescue—all our problems are instantly solved. We won't just be rescuing our mates; we'll have a witch to find mates for your sons when they've grown to manhood."

There's a small murmur through the crowd.

"It could still be a trap," Rajesh says, but he's gauging the shifting opinion of his lair of thirty-two dragons, mates, and children. Including his own mate, who holds their small son a little closer.

"If we don't take this risk," I say to them all, "none of our children have a future."

Rajesh scowls. *Yes,* I'm pushing it. But we're running out of time—

The mirror I have tucked inside my jacket buzzes. "Excuse me. I need to take this." I stride away from the group into one of the alcoves off the main ballroom. Alice's sweet face fills the mirror when I draw it out. "Hey, beautiful. How are things on your end?"

She does a double-take, and a small smile tugs at her lips. "Are you flattering me for some reason, Constantine?"

"Just stating the obvious." I glance at the crowd around Rajesh and Elizabeth. It's getting animated, and I want to give them a little time to sort that out. But not too much—we have to move on this. To Alice, I say, "This is a mirror, right? You should try looking in one sometime and seeing what I see."

"You're a fine thing yourself, but you don't see me telling you that."

"I think you just did." I can't help the grin.

"Can we discuss the rescue? Or do I need to embarrass myself further?" She does seem flustered, which brings a delightful pink to her cheeks. I tuck away the knowledge that not nearly enough men have told Alice how heart-stoppingly beautiful she is —something I intend to fix.

"We're nearly ready." I glance over, and Rajesh is looking somewhat disgruntled. I think he's been outvoted, and not just by Elizabeth. I return my gaze to Alice's lovely brown eyes. "In fact, we should get started. Are you ready for Niko to come get you?"

"Niko?" She's hesitating, which throws up alarm bells in my head.

"The Lord of our lair? He's a mated dragon, the kind that can teleport. He was part of both rescues." I'm trying to fathom why it matters who comes for her. "Is this not a good time?"

"It's a fine time." She bites her lip. "Will you be coming along? I'd be a bit more comfortable if you were."

"Of course." That protective instinct surges up. I'm the one she gave the mirror to—I'm the one she trusts. It makes sense to have me be the one to usher Alice through this. But that's not why it's tightening me up in anticipation. *I make her comfortable.* I've known enough women with enough trauma to know how big of a deal that is. "Give me five minutes. Then I'll be right by your side."

Her eyes light up in a way that's far too satisfying. *Fuck.* I need to tamp down this rapidly escalating romance I'm having with her. She whispers the portal closed, and I just stare at the black mirror for a moment.

Alice is probably the one woman in the world I *shouldn't* seduce. At least not while we're getting this operation underway. A little flirtation? *Yes.* Some light banter to build trust and make sure everything goes according to plan? *Absolutely.* But those heated looks I can't help giving her? *Fuck no.* And besides, it's possible one of these soul mates we're rescuing is mine. Until this moment, I've kept that thought far, far away. I've got baggage there I don't want to face —I didn't think I would have to, honestly, so I've kept it safely tucked away in the *Things Constantine Doesn't Fucking Think About* locker. Which gets me through the day. That and seducing possible soul mates, having plenty of outstanding sex to pass the time, and occasionally, being the hero who can rescue a woman who's been abused by the world and permanently ruin the day of the men who abused them.

Flirting with Alice is dangerous enough—I can get lost in a woman like her. But *actually* finding my soul mate? I'm not sure I'm ready. Or that I ever will be.

I push that thought aside—I've been successfully ignoring that possibility for two hundred years. And now it looks like Rajesh is resigned to whatever his lair has decided, so it's time to get this show on the road.

I trot back to him and the group. "What do you think? Can we count on you?"

"You have the support of the South Asian Lair," he says.

Sounds grudging, but I'll take it. "Great! We're gathering in Ireland, far from the lairs, so those aren't compromised. I can guide you there." I offer my hand for him to clasp. Rajesh is mated—he can teleport us both there, with my knowledge of where we're going. "Ready when you are."

He sighs, takes my hand, and a moment later, we're standing in a gorgeous green meadow that overlooks the ocean. Tall sandstone bluffs are battered by the water, sprouting their own greenery nestled in a fine, misty spray. We could have gathered anywhere on the planet, but I urged Niko to pick this enchanting Irish meadow because of Alice and her brogue. I'm not even from here, yet its natural beauty feels as restorative as the Greek Isles are for me—as long as I stay far from the charred ruins of our ancestral lair.

The knee-high grass is being tamped down by dozens of dragons. The site is remote enough, we shouldn't have any tourists stumbling upon us. I bid Rajesh goodbye, and he disappears, off to guide the rest of his lair here. They've only just joined us, so I imagine it might take them a few minutes to get organized—especially with all those kids someone needs to care for.

I hunt down Niko. Mated dragons are disappearing and reappearing with unmated dragons all over the meadow, but most of the Northern and European lairs appear to be here.

"South Asian Lair is in," I say to Niko as I stride up. "They'll be here shortly."

"Excellent." He's visually checking the crowd, probably counting heads.

"Alice is ready for us to fetch her. She wants me to come with you." I say it brusquely, hoping he won't read too much into it.

He just lifts his eyebrows and says nothing.

I wrestle with keeping the words in, but we're just delaying. "I make her comfortable."

His eyebrows lift higher.

"For fuck's sake, can we go?" I shouldn't let it rile me. Then again, he's not wrong about something going on between the two of us. At least on my end—I'm not at all sure where Alice stands. And I have to be careful—I don't know what the Vardigah have done to her. I don't want to unintentionally hurt her. That would be really *not okay* with me.

Niko clasps his hand on my shoulder. "Take good care of our witch, Constantine."

Right. All of dragonkind has a stake in Alice. I give him a short nod, and we're suddenly leaving the meadow and landing in her workshop. During the last rescue, we did a hell of a lot of damage in a short time—to be fair, most of it was caused by the Vardigah—but you'd never know it. The huge workbench in the middle is back in place with all its tins and jars. The chair where we found Julia is empty and the bindings are gone.

My heart lurches when I don't see Alice. I exchange a quick frown with Niko—we didn't even bring our fucking fireproof suits—and I don't think we want to call out for her. I wave him toward the front of the workshop while I edge toward the back. There's not really anywhere to go, but a couple alcoves are tucked behind the expansive book-shelves. Last time, I didn't pause to check out the library, so I run a glance across the books as I creep past. They're ancient, leather-bound, and there's not a speck of dust on them. Well used, I guess.

I reach the end, and Alice runs out from behind the last bookcase.

She nearly crashes into me. *"Oh!"* She blinks, then smiles. "I didn't expect you so quick." Now I'm intrigued as to what she was doing, but she hustles past me to the workbench. "Just a moment." She grabs an iron-and-copper goblet and gulps down something that makes her wince and then cough. Niko comes up behind her with a bewildered look that probably matches the one on my face. Alice wipes her mouth with the back of her hand and raises the goblet to us briefly before setting it down. "For stamina."

"Is that what wine does for you?" I'm wrestling with my grin—now that I'm paying attention, the workshop smells like mulled, spicy cider, but not a very good one.

"The wine just makes the potion go down." She

gives a shy nod to Niko but turns to face me. "Completing a pairing can be a bit challenging. According to the books. I figured I could use reinforcements."

Now that I've eased closer, I can see the dilation of her eyes. "How many of these reinforcements have you had?" I flick a look to Niko, who has a mounting concern on his face. A drunk witch was not part of the plan.

Alice scoffs. "It'd take a little more wine than that to get me hammered, Constantine. Don't we have some dragons to pair?"

I hold out my hand. "Any time you're ready."

She slips her hand into mine, and because I'm an idiot, I pull her in close and wrap my arms around her, holding her back to my chest. I hear the small gasp, but she tries to cover it. It just feels right to hold her. By the look on Niko's face, I'm fucking this *all* up, but he says nothing, just stands next to us and clasps his hand on my shoulder, then teleports us out of the workshop and back to the meadow.

He quickly steps away, giving us room.

"Holy shite," Alice breathes. She twists in my arms and beams up at me. "You've brought me home!" Then she's out of my arms and dashing across the meadow, toward the cliffs, holding the

skirts of her dress, her cape and hood and long red hair flying behind her. She slows as she nears the edge, which is good because I was starting to think she would leap straight off. Then she stops, plants her feet wide, and throws her arms out as if to embrace the sea. *"God, I missed you, Ireland!* Aren't you a sight for sore eyes?" She tips her head back, face to the sun, eyes closed, breathing the misty air deep as I trot up to her side.

I'm barely able to contain my grin. "Well, that was quite an entrance."

She smiles before she opens her eyes. "It's glorious." Then she opens them and turns to throw her arms around me, hugging her head tight to my chest. I'm so startled, I barely remember to hug her back. Just as I do, her sneak attack is over, and she's pulling back. "Thank you." She suddenly gets shy, dipping her head and stepping back. Only then does she seem to notice the entire meadow filled with people, all now openly staring at her. The breeze carries away their whispers, which is good because I'm sure they're chattering about her.

"Oh." Her voice is soft, and her eyes wide. "Well. This is… a lot to take in." She gives me a sideways glance. "Could be a challenge. Let's give it a go." Then she marches away from the cliff.

I hurry to her side as she steps through the tall grass. "How do you want to do this?"

She slows as she nears the closest dragon—it's Saryn, son of Renn and Ketu. I last saw him at Julia's bedside, looking as uncomfortable and slightly terrified as he does now.

"Might as well have them line up." She steps up to Saryn. "All right. Never done this before, but I figure neither have you?"

He shakes his head.

"You got a name?" she asks.

"Saryn." He coughs on the dryness. "Saryn Blackscale."

"Saryn Blackscale." She raises her hand, and Saryn's alarm steps up two levels. "I'm not gonna hex you, Saryn Blackscale. But I *do* need to put my hand on your forehead for a bit. It's not complicated, according to the books. Just a touch on the head, a brief incantation, and the identity of your soul mate should appear in your mind. It'll take a little magic, but sure, that's why I'm here. With my reinforcements."

Saryn dashes a look to me.

"She means magic reinforcements," I say.

He gives her a look just short of terror.

"Are you ready, then?" she asks cheerily.

I think none of us are, including Alice. She's not quite slurring her words, but there's a drunken happiness that's dulled the edges a little. And I like her edges. It worries me, but not enough to stop her.

Saryn nods, jerkily, then seems to steel himself.

"Let's give this a shot." Alice places one hand on Saryn's shoulder—I think to steady herself—and lays the other palm-flat on his forehead. Then she whispers low in a sing-song cadence.

"*Not time nor land,*
nor sea contain.
Not death nor life
nor soul remain.
When two hearts beat,
their broke souls cry.
Ever more, now,
till now they die."

Saryn gasps. "Wait... I... can you see that?" He's staring at nothing.

Alice's gaze is likewise distant. "That lovely vision of your dragon-spirited mate? Yeah." She grins. "Can you feel it? The pull of where she is?"

"Yeah." Saryn breathes the word. "But I already know where she is."

"You've met her, then?" She drops her hand and leans back to look Saryn in the face.

He turns to me with wide eyes. "It's Julia. The one you rescued."

"*What?*" I was so focused on finding the captured soul mates, I forgot about the one we'd already brought back. Plus, there are many more soul mates in the world than those who've been taken by the Vardigah. Will Alice sense them all? *Of course, she will.* I don't know why this is short-circuiting my brain, but as I gaze out at the field of dragons, I realize... she will pair every single one of them. Today. Right now.

Including me.

"Go on, now." Alice waves away a tentatively grinning Saryn. He peels off, and the next dragon steps up. "And you are?" she asks him.

"Kass." He's wide-eyed, flicking a look at Saryn's retreating back. "Are you really going to..."

"Not unless you step up." She beckons him closer, then places her hand on his forehead. She sings her short song—it's more like a poem, not quite an incantation—and shock blossoms on Kass's face.

"Is she all right?" he demands, pulling away from Alice's hand.

"Last I saw." Then she drops her hand. "Her name is Kirsten." Then Alice sways a little as if she's unsteady on her feet.

I immediately slip one hand to the small of her back and hold her hand with the other. "You okay?"

"Ah sure, I'm grand." She smiles at me, and it's radiant—she's *happy*, I realize. I don't know if it's the wine or the sea bluffs and the emerald field... or the fact that she's using her Gift to connect dragons to their soul mates. Whatever it is, it makes her beauty shine even brighter.

She stands stronger on her own, and I let her go. Besides, the next dragon is eager for his turn.

"My name's Petr," he says as he quickly steps up to her.

She repeats the hand-to-forehead connection and whispers the spell a little louder. I watch her more closely this time—she closes her eyes as she recites the words, then opens them and seems to see into eternity. Or some other realm.

Petr's face transforms into awe. "She's so beautiful." I've never seen love so plainly on a man's face.

Alice grips his shoulder, her other palm still planted on his forehead. "Can you *feel* it?"

"The connection. *Yes,*" he breathes.

A tremor flashes through my heart. Is this what

I will look like when Alice connects me to my soul mate? Or… will it be something much worse?

"All right, Petr, listen up." She's holding him with both hands on his shoulders now. "She's not with the Vardigah, thank Christ. But we'll still need you for the rescue. You hear me? No running off after her right away, not until we're finished with this business."

Torment springs to life on Petr's face.

"I know, I know," Alice says. "But I need your word. Your brother dragons need your help. And you wouldn't hesitate if you'd seen what the Vardigah are doing to these poor women."

"Right. Of course." He nods shakily. Alice releases him, and he wanders off.

The next dragon is already stepping up. There are dozens to get through—close to fifty at my last count—but she takes time with each one. Some are mated to the captured women. Some have mates roaming free in the world somewhere—but the men now know *where*. One of the older dragons has a soul mate who is still a child—she must have lived several lifetimes, coming back each time to try again. He'll have to wait, but I can tell by the hope in his eyes that it doesn't matter to him how long; he'll be there when she's ready. As the line shortens,

Alice seems to be gripping the dragons a little more tightly as she casts her spell. Twice, I have to brace her again as a wave of dizziness seems to overcome her.

"Make sure you wait to find her," Alice says as she dismisses one of the South Asian dragons.

Then she steps back and nearly tips over.

I've been hovering close, so I'm right there to catch her. "Okay, that's enough."

"I'm not done." She pushes against my hold, but she doesn't even have her feet under her.

I slip my arm around her waist. "It's wearing on you." It's obvious.

She grips my arm and looks up at me. "There are women, captured ones, who haven't been paired." The dilation in her eyes is gone—whatever potion she drank has long since worn off. Dark shadows under her eyes make it seem like she hasn't slept for days.

"You can't keep going like this," I insist.

"I have to." She says it plainly, but then closes her eyes and rests her head against my arm. "Just three more," she whispers. "Three more, and we'll be able to find them all."

"Come on, sit down." I ease her into the grass with me. She folds her legs, but they were barely holding her up, anyway. I brace her so she can sit upright in the grass, her cloak a blanket under her, then scoot forward so she can rest her back against my chest.

The next dragon kneels down so she can reach him.

She keeps going. Eyes half-closed. Lips barely whispering the incantation. She doesn't have to say anything to the dragons as they approach—the entire field knows the drill by now. Alice just touches them, says her spell, and whatever magic she's conjuring exacts a price from her… but the dragons lift to their feet with love and hope in their eyes. As she fades even more, I wrack my brain for why these last few women seem to have no matches with the men here. It slowly dawns on me there are all kinds of dragons not present. The children back at the lairs. The guardians left to watch over them—although most of those have rotated out and tele-ported here. The mated dragons are ferrying everyone home as soon as they've been paired, so the field is quickly emptying out. And then there are the rogue dragons, who don't belong to any lair, and the ones in the Chinese lair who we've lost contact with—any of those could be mates for the captured women.

Alice dismisses a dragon, then twists to me, her bleary eyes up at mine. "Only one left. We can stop. I can find her for you."

Thank God. "All right." I beckon the next dragon in line—there are still seven left. "You and the others will have to wait. She can't do anymore."

I don't know him—he's one of the European dragons—but he seems utterly crushed.

Alice's eyes are closed, her head leaned back against my shoulder, but she taps me with her hand. "Tell him, I promise I'll pair them," she whispers. "I just need… a little rest…"

I jerk my head to wave them off. They drag their feet about it, but slowly they break up and wander over to the mated dragons who teleport them away, one by one. Finally, it's just Niko left with Alice and me in the meadow.

He frowns hard at the shape Alice is in. "She all right to go back?"

I'm doubtful about it, too.

"Not yet." Alice's eyes open, and she pulls in a deep breath. "I still need to pair Constantine." Then she twists in my arms like she's going to turn right around and plant that magic hand of hers on my head.

To Niko, I say, "Give us a minute. I'll text you when I need you."

His eyebrows lift again, but then he teleports away, leaving us alone in the meadow. Alice is still working on turning around to face me.

I slip my hand into hers to stop her. "We don't need any more pairs. You said it yourself. You can take us to the last soul mate." Odds are that last unpaired soul mate isn't even mine. But I've already thought this through—I'm going on this mission, and I'm making sure Alice makes it back *out* of the Vardigah realm when we leave.

"I can do it," she says, eyes earnest. "Don't you want to know your soul mate?"

"No," I say. "I really don't."

SIX

Alice

CONSTANTINE ISN'T MAKING SENSE.

My head's so wrecked with all the matchmaking, I'm certain I haven't heard him right. "You're talking rubbish, Constantine." I blink and peer at his beautiful face. He's been getting me through, concern in his words and strength in his arms. I'll be the first to admit I don't *want* to pair him—I don't want to see that connection, that *love*, he'll have for his soul mate when the magic is made. My greedy heart wants to keep him for myself. But I can't deny the man his destiny. "What dragon doesn't want to find his mate?"

"One who got her killed the first time."

I squint at him. Another wave of fatigue washes

through me. *"Jaysus,* I need to lie down for this story."

His smile is gentle as I brace myself down into the grass, rolling onto my back where my cape and hood make a decent blanket. I gaze up at the stunning blue sky, where the clouds are as puffy and white as spring lambs cavorting across the heavens. Constantine lies down next to me, snuggling up in a way that would have me all heated if I weren't as tired as the dead.

He props his head up to peer down at me. "You don't want to hear this story."

More like he doesn't want to tell it. "You think I don't know my own mind?"

He smiles. "Not at all."

"Then, don't make me ask again." Lying down feels good—next to Constantine, even better. The field and the sky are working a spell to heal the drain of all the pairing. But those pairings brought a certain joy as well—*finally,* I've done a good thing. If only the women can be liberated, all these dragons today will build new families. There's no tearing that away. No burning it down. I will have always done *this thing,* no matter what comes next… and it is good.

Now to set Constantine on his way, and I'll be

done. The Vardigah can have me, for as long as that lasts. They can't force me to undo what I've done here today. I'll drink nightshade before I let that happen.

Constantine's smile has faded. "You know our ancestral lair was burned to the ground by the Vardigah. They tried to wipe us out."

"In fact, I didn't know." I sigh and glance at the beauty of the grass. So much like home. The fatigue somehow makes it easier to confess my shame. "I grew up in a village in a field like this one." I look back to Constantine and his suddenly-sharp eyes. "It's like a dream to me now. All the fights and all the love. It seemed there were endless cousins and aunts and neighbors, but I think the village was less than fifty, all told. It was my home. And the Vardigah burned it to the ground. I suppose we have that in common."

His expression softens. "How old were you?"

"Seven." Even now, it seems impossible—that I've been with the Vardigah these thirteen years.

The shock passes his face like a wave—shock, horror, then a rage I understand all too well. *"Alice."* His voice is thick, like the words can't squeeze past the anger.

I understand that too. "Being so young… they

thought I would forget. And for a time, I did. To my shame, I believed their lies—that it was the dragons who destroyed my family. My home. That it was the Vardigah who rescued me. That they snatched what they could of my mother's books from the fire. Only later, when I actually *read* the books, did I discover the truth—about them and about you." I touch his cheek. There's so much happening in his shifting expressions. So much he's not saying, but I feel it, regardless. "How could you be our enemies when we were made to bring you love?"

He captures my hand against his cheek then turns… *and kisses my palm.* That banishes the fatigue and sends the flutter right back in my belly. Then he holds my hand in his, between us.

"You have no idea," he says softly, "what you've done today. You've saved us."

"All except you." I smile and lift my eyebrows, but he has my hand trapped, and he's not letting go so I can use it. But he nods and clears his throat, so I'm patient.

"I'd already been paired before the attack," he says, looking at our joined hands. "I was young, barely twenty-five." He lifts his gaze to my face. "Probably older than you, but it was different then. Not just because I thought I had all the time in the world—the whole world was different. The pairing happened, and I felt that connection. Just like these dragons here today. Back then, it was expected you'd go out into the world and find her. Romance your mate until she fell in love. Then you would reveal yourself, your dragon world, your family. And then and only then would you seduce her into bed. The mating wouldn't happen unless she was truly in love with you, and you couldn't risk a baby before then—she wouldn't survive it. So the order of things was important. But of course, I was impatient." Then he stops the story, and I have to hold back from striking the man.

Instead, I guess. "You had your wicked way with her. I'm not gonna lie, Constantine—it wouldn't take much to talk a woman into your bed."

A smile grows slowly on his face until it feels like he's beaming it upon me. "Could I talk you into my bed?"

"Sure," I say because it's definitely in the realm of possibilities. "Your problem would be getting me *out.*"

He laughs, and I love the sound of it. But it's a bit of bragging on my part. I've read *all* my mother's books, including the ones with the erotic arts, and I've taken the edge off loneliness with my own hand plenty, but this right here in the grass is the closest I've been to lying with a man.

When Constantine's humor settles a little, I add, "Never mind I've no experience at all."

His eyes sparkle. "I have plenty to share."

I cock my head. "Your soul mate might have something to say about that."

He looks away.

"Tell me, Constantine," I say. "Or let me put my palm to your head."

He's still gazing at the grass. "Her name was Zoe, and I was absolutely smitten the moment we were paired. I rushed headlong to her—she wasn't far, just in Athens." He brings that gaze back to mine. "I was foolish and young and could barely keep my hands off her. But she was a nobleman's daughter and wasn't going to fall in love with some bright-eyed commoner who was far too eager to kiss her. My brilliant plan was to reveal myself—to show my dragon form—then bring her back to the lair and romance her there. Surely *then* she would fall in love with me."

"Seems reasonable." I frown. "I guess… I just assumed soul mates fell naturally in love."

He smiles, but there's pain behind it. "Usually. But not always. If a dragon can't win his mate's heart, he has to wait. She'll live her life—possibly with someone else—and when she dies, she'll be reborn, and he'll have another chance."

"What a horrible thing." I can't help the curling of my lip.

He shrugs one shoulder. "It's better than only having one chance. Which for me…" He shakes his head and stares off into the grass again. "I'd brought her to the lair. I was utterly *failing* at romancing her. She was mostly terrified. And stubborn. In fact, she was marching out the gates of the lair's castle when the attack began. I tried to save her, of course—I shifted and sheltered her with my body. It didn't matter. The Vardigah's magical fire was too intense, turning everything into ash. I was the only survivor—and then only barely, and only because I was outside the gates at the edge of the inferno. Zoe was still human. We were still unmated. She had no protection except my worthless hide." He stops again, and I almost regret forcing him to recall it.

"If you'd mated, would that have been better?" I ask gently.

He pulls his gaze in to meet mine. "That's the irony. If we'd been mated, we would have both died. I often wish that had been the case, honestly.

But no… *my* shame is that she shouldn't have been there at all." He smiles a little and traces a finger along my cheek. "So, you see, my sweet Alice, I've already been paired. And failed to win my mate's love. And managed to get her killed. I can't help thinking that's why, in all this time, I've never found her. I don't think she wants to be found. And I'm not sure I should really go looking."

My heart is breaking for this beautiful man. "But she's *reborn,*" I say because despite this guilt he carries—and I can understand that—it doesn't make much sense to run away from love. "Can't you start over? I mean… will she remember?"

"No."

"Then what's holding you back?"

He just sighs and looks at me like he's weighing whether to give in or fight me more. He's looming above me—close enough to dip down and kiss, but that's not going to happen if I show him his soul mate. I know that. And as much as I'd like my first —and probably last and only—kiss to be with this lovely man, I'll not be adding to his guilt. I raise my palm and hold it ready.

"Sophia," I proclaim. "She's the last woman being held by the Vardigah. She could be your soul mate."

"I'm coming with you to rescue her, regardless," he says with a small smile.

"All the better."

He stares at my palm for a long moment, then pulls in a breath and lets it out. "I *should* know," he says quietly. He looks to me. "In case she's in danger."

"Exactly so." I move slow but place my palm on his forehead just like all the dragons before. I say a silent goodbye to the possibility of keeping Constantine for myself, even for a short while. But it feels right to do this, even if he's squeezed his eyes shut like this will physically hurt him. Then I say the ancient words, the poetry that opens the connection between souls—a dragon's and his mate's—and hold my breath for the vision to come.

It doesn't.

I know I'm tired, but... I say the incantation a second time. And again, I wait. But there's no vision, no far-off flash of insight, just Constantine's face looming above me with his lips pressed so tight they've lost all color.

I pull my hand back.

Constantine opens his eyes. "It didn't work."

I can't explain it, so I just shrug against my cloak in the grass.

He sighs. "I told you. She doesn't want to be found."

"That can't be right," I protest. "Finding love for others is my purpose—it's in my blood. The books talk endlessly about it. The irony of it is I know nothing of love myself. But I can tell you— this never happens. If a dragon lives, so does his mate's dragon spirit. She should keep seeking you until your spirit passes into the next realm. I don't understand—"

"It's all right, Alice." He puts his hand to my cheek, bending down a little to smile at me. "Maybe this is how it's meant to be."

I scowl because that *can't* be right, but then I don't hardly mind at all that he's looking at me the way he is.

"Do you know how beautiful you are?" His gaze rests on my lips more than my eyes. And it can't be my imagination that he's moved even closer.

Suddenly, the flutter is making demands. It's saying this is what's meant to be and to stop wasting time about it.

"Will you give us a kiss?" I ask, my cheeks hot with the request. "Never been, you know."

"Never?" His beautiful eyes sparkle.

"Well, my cousin kissed me when we were five,

but I punched him for it, so I figure that doesn't count."

His face lights up with a smile, and he has a laugh with that, but then he leans in, and just when I think he's going to kiss me, he doesn't. His cheek slides along mine, and he whispers in my ear. "A kiss is shared, not given, sweet Alice."

"I've got one to share, then." I can hardly catch a breath.

He pulls away, but just enough to bring his lips to my cheek. He brushes along, not a proper kiss, just a touch. It sets my entire being afire. I pull in a shuddering breath then his lips find mine. His kiss is sweet and soft, and I hardly know what to do in response. But then his tongue sneaks out, and my mouth opens for him, as if it knows what it's doing. I'm still awkward until he invades my mouth proper… and then it's like my soul opens, and I'm lost. My hands clutch at his shoulders. My tongue's dancing with his. I feel *explored* in a way that's unmoored me—like I've given myself over to him already, mouth on mouth, bodies grappling, the weight of him pressing me into the grass. I grab at his back with abandon. I don't care about anything but the *feel* of him—strong like a mountain clad in silk—and the *taste* of him—earthy and musky and entirely masculine.

My hands are just working into that long, gorgeous hair when he shudders against me and gasps into my mouth. Then he pulls away. A small whimper escapes me—my sudden need for him is total and embarrassing.

He's gazing down at me in surprise.

I want to ask, *"What's wrong?"* but even those words can't make it out of my mouth.

"I don't understand," he mutters, then looks at me, *really looks*, scouring my face and my body, like he's seeing me for the first time. Something catches his eye—my arm lying on the grass beside my head, where it fell after he pulled away.

"What's that?" He frowns and reaches for my arm, where the sleeve has slid down and exposed it. I look because I have no idea what he means. He runs his thumb over the mark the Vardigah gave me long ago—when they first kidnapped me and laid waste to the rest of my family and home.

It's a simple X because the Vardigah aren't poetic. "They tagged me," I tell him. "It's like a magical tattoo. When they first captured me, I think the Vardigah weren't quite sure what to make of me, a child witch." Constantine releases me, and I miss his touch immediately. But there's concern on his face, so I explain. "Witches come into most of their powers later, in adolescence. But the Vardigah couldn't know that. They thought I might conjure a way out of their realm and run away. They told me it was for my protection. Bloody lies, of course."

He's scowling. "What does the mark do?"

"It's their way of turning a *person* into a *thing*. Remember how I said they can only transport to a place they know? A physical location?" I hold up the mark. "This is a *thing* they know."

His eyes go wide in alarm. "Like right now, they could find you here and come for you?"

"Yes." I frown because I thought I explained, but I guess not. "That's why I wanted us far from the lairs."

"So, they could be here any minute."

"Well, yes." He's sitting up in alarm, so I prop myself. "I knew we had a bit of time. Jarod was off on some important matter. But you're right. I should be getting back."

He still seems upset. "I didn't think you'd be going back until the raid."

"Oh, no, I can't stay away that long." I frown because I have no sense of how long I've been gone. "They'll be checking on me sooner than that."

He scrambles up to standing and pulls his phone out of his pocket. I sit all the way up, making sure the dizziness is gone. Then I climb to my feet, brushing the grass from my cape. Disappointment is weighing down my heart, but what did I expect? That kiss was more than I had a right to hope for.

Niko appears by Constantine's side. "Ready to go?" he asks me.

"I suppose." My heart's truly constricting now. I console myself that I *will* see Constantine again— they need me to rescue Sophia, and he's already promised to come.

Constantine takes my hand but only to show the mark to Niko. "The Vardigah are tracking her."

"What? *Shit.*" He scowls. "So, I should take her back, right? Before they find she's gone."

"We need some way to *break* it," Constantine insists.

"*Break* it?" Niko glances at the mark. "We don't even know what it is."

"We have to or she can't—" Constantine stops and gives me a panicked look.

I can't *what?* "What are you after?" I ask him.

"*Alice.*" He takes both my hands in his. "We need to get you free of the Vardigah." He seems tormented by this.

"Not bloody likely." I just blink as it dawns on me—he means to keep me. All the dragons do. I would be their pet witch, instead of the Vardigah's. Not that I'd mind as such—my people and his have always lived side-by-side, mutually beneficial in our arts—but my heart is crying.

Because for a moment, I thought it might be something more.

"There has to be a way," Constantine insists, half to me and half to his friend.

"There never was." I step back, slipping out of his hand-holding. "I've done my good work here," I say thickly, "but this was only ever going to end one way."

"What?" The horror on Constantine's face makes my heart hurt.

I turn to Niko. "It's time I go back. Come for me in the raid. I'll show you the way to—" Then a sudden blast throws us from our feet. Before I can even recover my senses, a Vardigah transports to my side and clamps an iron hand on me, hauling me up to standing.

Niko and Constantine have sprung up, but there are half a dozen Vardigah in the field surrounding us. Niko transports just in time to avoid a blast of fire that scorches the field. He reappears by

Constantine's side only to have both disappear before another volley of fire can reach them. Its magical blue flames roll across the grass, leaving charred earth behind until it meets the bluff and falls over.

The Vardigah releases me, and Jarod strides up. *"It is fortunate we could rescue you,"* he says in Elvish. His ears are twitching, which could be agitation or suspicion.

There's so much I want to say. That he's wrong. That I know all the lies. That I hate everything his people have done to mine and to the dragons. But I hold my tongue one last time. Once I've drunk the nightshade potion, and Jarod can no longer determine my fate... *then* I will speak my mind.

"I could not resist them," I say to him. Which is more true than the dark elf will ever know. *"They overpowered me."*

"Do you have knowledge of their lair?" All the Vardigah are keen on this answer.

"They only brought me here." Also true.

Jarod signals the others, and in an instant, we're leaving the field to return to the Vardigah realm.

SEVEN

Constantine

"WE HAVE TO GO *BACK.*" I GRIP NIKO BY THE shoulders when I realize we've left Alice behind. "What the *fuck,* Niko!" He's returned us to the Northern Lair, to his office. We're alone.

"We couldn't take her with us." He pulls out of my grip, but gently. Like he's not sure I'm entirely stable.

Which I'm not. *"Gah!"* I fist my hands and pound them to my forehead.

"We can get her before—"

"She's my soul mate!" I blurt out, hands thrown in frustration.

Niko leans back, eyeing me even more warily. "She told you that?"

"No, I *felt* it!" Dammit, why doesn't he believe

me? We don't have time to mess around with this. *"I kissed her,* Niko. And I damn well know what it feels like to kiss your soul mate." He knows about Zoe. It was just him and Aleks and me in the beginning. The two of them nursed me back to health after the fire. We built the North Lair together. We go all the way back. He cannot fucking doubt me now.

"She's a witch, Constantine." He says it like I'm an idiot who doesn't realize that.

I try to calm the raging panic in my chest. "Look, I know it's unusual for a witch and a dragon—"

"I've literally never of—"

"Niko." I grit my teeth. "It doesn't matter. I'm telling you, I'm going to save her from the Vardigah if it fucking kills me."

Niko puts up his hands. "All right." He's still looking askance at me. "I want her out of their clutches too—she's the only witch we've got."

Finally. I rub my face with both hands, wiping away the frustration. "How do we destroy this tag they've put on her?"

"No fucking clue." Niko's phone buzzes and he checks it. "And we've got zero time to figure it out. We're almost ready for the raid."

"We need Alice to get Sophia." I grip my hair with both hands, ready to pull it out. How the fuck can I break this Vardigah spell they have over her?

"True," Niko says. "And I'll be the one taking you both there. But I can't bring her back here. Not with that tracker." He gives me a pointed look. Because we can't take Alice *anywhere* with the tracker. They'll just come for her. And destroy whoever's in their path. "I don't know what you're thinking," he adds, "but you can't get caught by the Vardigah, either. I know Alice has been keeping secrets from them, but they've got a fucking mind probe, Constantine. Alice said as much, right? They're hoping to capture one of us. So they can find the lairs."

Fuck. He's right.

"And I'm really sorry to hear she's your mate," Niko says carefully.

I narrow my eyes. "What the fuck are you saying?"

He grimaces. "Remember when you thought Alice was a threat to us all?"

"That was before I knew—"

"You were right." He presses his lips together.

That stops me cold.

And then I lunge for him.

My hands are immediately around his throat—literally no thought has crossed my brain, it just happened—but Niko's a mated dragon, with a mated dragon's strength, and he easily wrenches out of my grasp and shoves me back. He's not even trying, and I go staggering, catching myself on his desk to keep from falling.

"I don't like saying it," he grinds out.

My chest is heaving—not from the fight, but from the idea that *he's right*. *"Niko…"* I'm choking. "I can't lose her again. Not like this. *Not to them." Fuck*, I'm barely holding it together.

Niko, my brother dragon, strides across the room and grabs me into a hug. "I know. My brother, *I know.*" And I believe him. *He's mated now.* All this time, these two centuries, there were only a few dragons who could truly understand my loss. To have been paired, to have that connection, only to have it ripped away. The unmated dragons could envision it—fantasize about it—but they couldn't know the soul-ripping that happens when anything at all threatens your mate. *Much less kills her in your arms.* Only the mated dragons had any idea, and for them, it was utterly unthinkable. They would literally die when their mate did.

Which is what Niko is saying has to happen.

Alice has to die. Her dragon spirit has to be released. Her witching powers have to be kept out of the Vardigah's hands. The only problem? I'd sooner take my own life. Or kill any dragon who tried to harm her. Probably both.

Niko pulls back and holds me by the shoulders. "I know this is hard, but we've got to focus on the greater good of the lair—of our people, Constantine."

I nod, dully. All the fight has gone out of me.

"We can't decide anything about Alice right now," he says. "We've got twenty-five soul mates to rescue. I've got twenty-five mated dragons ready to risk their lives to make that happen and another fifty unmated dragons ready to do the same. This is a huge and risky operation. I've ordered some of the unmated dragons—a few that Alice has already paired to women *not* held by the Vardigah—to stay behind with the kids. We need someone to keep the species going in case all of this goes up in flames. Including me. And you. And maybe Alice. For all we know, they've already—"

My head snaps up. "She's not dead."

He nods. "You'd probably feel it, I agree. But we're racing the clock here. We need to execute this mission *now.*"

He's right. But it's tearing me apart. "All right." I breathe through the pain of it. "Let's do this. But if I can't save her, Niko…" I don't know what I'll do.

"First things first." His voice is rough. "Execute the mission. Then we'll figure out what to do about Alice." He jabs a finger in my face. "No heroics. No getting caught by the Vardigah. Do I make myself clear?"

I nod. Because I can't save my soul mate if I'm in the same trap she is. And trying to save her while dooming my people is a coward's choice.

"Okay, let's go." Niko teleports us to the main floor, where all seventy-five dragons are gathered. Everyone's putting on flame-proof suits, just like the two missions before.

Niko hustles off to check in with everyone. As I pay closer attention, I see the dragons are actually gathered into teams of three—one mated dragon and two unmated ones. I recognize the ones Alice said were paired with the captured women—there's one in each team. It's a room full of men eager to risk their lives to save their soul mates.

Why can't I be allowed to do the same? Why the fuck am I cursed?

I find Saryn already suited up and handing out

helmets. He fetches me a suit, and I slowly pull it on, numbly fastening the closures and desperately trying to figure out how to break elvish magic I don't even understand. I can't think of a thing other than Alice's lovely face... and how I *can't* save her.

Again.

EIGHT

Alice

———————

I HAVE TO FOCUS TO KEEP MY HAND FROM SHAKING.

It's pressed to Sophia's forehead. I'm supposed to be checking on her dragon spirit. In truth, I'm in a complete panic. When will the raid happen? Will Constantine still come for me? I'm constantly surrounded by guards—Jarod's not leaving me alone for even a second now. Sophia is the third woman he's dragged me to, making me watch while he torments them, trying to destroy the dragon spirit within.

Sophia's is hanging on by a thread. I'm stretching this out as long as I—

"*Is it present?*" Jarod demands, looming right behind me and making me jump.

"*Yes.*"

Jarod roars his frustration and yanks me back. The technicians swarm in to administer more pain.

Sophia screams, and it's all I can do to keep in the tears. I'm terrified if he keeps going, he'll succeed—which means a dragon will die. And if he doesn't, he may just kill the women to keep the dragons from coming for them. Which would at least let the dragons live.

It's a horrific choice.

One I'm prepared to make *for myself*—dying so the dragons may live—but not for anyone else.

Jarod waves off the technicians. To me, he barks, *"Again."*

I've never seen him so angry. I hustle forward and make a show of checking for Sophia's dragon spirit.

She's frowning up at me with pain-bleary eyes. "Make it stop. *Please."*

I can barely keep the tears in. The Vardigah won't understand what she's saying, but they'll know the tone. The fear and pain in her voice. And my tears are giving me away.

I take a moment to duck my head and wipe my eyes, then I turn to Jarod with my head held high. *"I want this one as my assistant."*

He cocks his head. *"Is it dead?"* He means her dragon-spirit.

"Yes."

Jarod huffs out something that must be celebration. Or frustration.

"I want her," I repeat. *"She's no use to you."*

"Take her." He waves this off as if it's unimportant. My heart leaps—*yes!*—but then he jabs a long finger at me. *"The others must die. Today. You will return."*

I nod my quick agreement. I only need a little time back at my workshop. Enough to make the potion. Enough to signal Constantine that he must come now. That Jarod will kill them all rather than let them fall into the dragons' hands. Jarod waves one technician to come with him. They both disappear, no doubt off to another cell to torment another woman.

"Release her," I say to the other technician. He takes a moment to retract all the mechanical restraints that come from beneath the torture chair.

"What's happening?" Sophia says, eyes wide and jittery.

"It's okay." I give her my hand once the restraints have freed her. "You're coming with me." She clasps my hand, but she's shakier than I am. I grip her hand harder and slide my arm around her waist, dipping my shoulder under hers to hold her up. She's so thin and light—the Vardigah haven't bothered to feed the women, so they just waste away. They would have died of thirst except I told Jarod early on to give them water or he wouldn't have time to destroy their dragon spirits. But food… that was too disgusting for the Vardigah to contemplate.

I nod to the technician that we're ready. He transports us back to my workshop. Sophia and I hobble-walk past my workbench and bookshelves and around the corner to my cot tucked in the back. She collapses into the bed and stays right where she slumped. I ask if she's okay, but she just whimpers, eyes squeezed shut. I step back from the bed and nearly bump into the technician.

"You come with me," he says, expression flat. *"The next one awaits."*

I gesture to Sophia's slumped form with both hands. *"She needs witch magic."*

"You come with me," he repeats.

"No." I turn my back on him, hustling to my workbench, praying he doesn't simply transport me to the next cell anyway. I pull out a pot and toss things in. *Beehive husk. Deer antler dust. Mountain flower.*

I'm just pulling random things from their tins. What I really need is the nightshade—ten berries of *atropa belladonna* are the true magic. The rest is just for show.

I find it in a special box I've kept wrapped in tissue and buried in a drawer.

The technician is watching me keenly.

I crush everything in the pot then add a full goblet of wine. I'll need it to dull out the horror as the hallucinations and convulsions set in. I have no idea how long it will take, but I suppose that doesn't matter. I'm stirring the pot without heat just to get through the performance part more quickly. Once it's mixed, I pour the deadly brew into my goblet, taking care to triple rinse out the pot. I don't know who might make a potion from my humble workshop in the future, but I wouldn't want to accidentally poison them. I start to carry the goblet to my cot, where Sophia is collapsed. The technician is following me, watching my every move.

I stop and turn to face him, offering the goblet. *"Do you want a drink?"*

He steps back, startled. *"No."*

I wave him back. *"Then stay here."* I'm hoping the general Vardigah suspicion—and vague fear—

of anything witchy, especially my potions, will keep him from following me to the cot.

It works. He stays by the workbench as I retreat around the corner of my bookcase. I have to make this fast—he'll come looking soon.

Sophia is crashed on my bed, curled up in a ball on top of half the blanket. I set the goblet on the floor and carefully pull the other half of the blanket over her. She keeps her eyes closed and burrows deeper into my pillow. She's in a bad way, but this is going to work. I'll take the potion, so I'll be on my way by the time the dragons arrive—but they *will* come for me, and they'll find Sophia here.

I settle on the floor next to the cot, my back braced against the edge, and take up the goblet. I stare at it a moment. It smells of sweetness and wine with an ashy scent from the other ingredients. Not the worst I've ever drunk. It shouldn't be hard going down—it's the *death* afterward that's the trick.

My mouth runs dry.

I wish... I spy the portal mirror on the cot, revealed by the shifting around of the blanket. I tell myself I only want to say goodbye, that it can't hurt —too much—and now's as good a time as any. I hold the goblet in one hand and the mirror in the other.

I whisper the words to open the portal.

Constantine answers right away. *"Alice!"* The creases at the corners of his eyes say he's been worrying about me.

It makes my heart glad and hurt at the same time. "Hey, beautiful. How are things on your end?" I smile at my own joke, repeating his words back.

"We're almost ready." He's in a rush, and he's got the strange suit on from before, when he came to rescue Cinder and then Julia. Maybe I'll still be here to see him in it when he comes.

Maybe I'll be dead before he gets here.

"You should come quick," I say. "Jarod's bent on killing all the women. But I've got Sophia here in my workshop." I hold the mirror up so he can see her curled form under the blanket. "So come here first, okay?"

"We're leaving in like…" He checks something past the mirror. "Thirty seconds."

I sigh. "That's enough time, I suppose."

His gaze sharpens at my tone. "Enough time for what?"

"To drink this down." I lift the cup to the mirror so he can see.

"What's that?" He sucks in a breath. "Tell me you found a potion to break the Vardigah's spell!"

"In a manner of speaking." It feels like everything is slowing down, and I haven't even taken a draught yet. "It's nightshade."

"Night… *nightshade?*" His eyes nearly pop out of his head. "That's poison!"

"You're bang on about that."

"What the fuck! *Alice.*" He looms closer in the mirror like he might leap through it.

I almost wish he could. Then again, he'd stop me, given the fury in his face.

"I can't let them use me, Constantine." It seems so easy to say, although the cup is surprisingly heavy in my hand. "You know it has to be like this."

"No! You can't… Alice… *please.*" He looks ready to cry.

Maybe this portal call wasn't such a good idea.

"I just wanted to tell you about Sophia—"

"Alice!"

"Yeah?" I'm running out of words.

"You're my soul mate." There's anguish on his face, and it ripples through my heart.

"Why would you say that?" He can't really believe—

"Because it's true."

"But you don't have…" I trail off because I'd forgotten—there was no soul mate for Constantine.

Which made no sense. "I mean, I couldn't find..."
Jesus, Mary, and Joseph.

"You couldn't find her," he says, a pained smile working its way in, *"because she's you."*

I blink. And set down the goblet because it's feckin' heavy, and I need to focus. "How is that possible?"

"I don't know." The anguish is back on his face. "But I can't lose you, Alice. *Not again.* There has to be another way."

A torrent of emotions takes hold in my chest, turning and spinning and tossing my heart around. Constantine's suffered too much. He should be mated. If it were any other woman, I'd send him to her, even if it broke my heart... *but if it's me?* I give the goblet a disgusted look. How can I do that to him?

"Alice! We're almost ready to come get you." He's talking fast now. "Don't do anything until I get there, okay? Promise me!"

I look at him through the portal. His desperate concern. His fervent plea. This man would risk everything—is about to risk his life— to come rescue me even though there's no hope in it. Even though he's no match against the Vardigah, not if they come for me. As they will unless we can break this hex they've put upon me.

I have only the vaguest memory of love. The sweet days of childhood. My mother's hugs. My father lifting me high in the air. I remember the cozy nights of stories by the bedside, and then the screams of that day of fire, when I lost everything. It was nothing but terror. Only later did I recall my mother hiding me in a cabinet. Telling me to be quiet. The sound of her pain as she died protecting me.

That's what I know of love—the people who love me, dying.

And here's a man ready to do it again.

Fuck no.

"There has to be another way," I whisper.

"Alice, are you ready?" Constantine's got his helmet on, visor up. "We're coming for you!"

"Come for me, my love."

His eyes go wide, but then someone's yelling at him. Behind him, I can see them—dozens and dozens of dragons in fireproof suits, disappearing in sets of three. Constantine flips down his visor, and the image tips up to the ceiling as he sets the mirror down.

I do likewise, scrambling to my feet and grabbing my goblet of poison. I march around the bookcase to find the Vardigah technician idly examining the boxes on my workbench.

"What are you doing?" I demand, marching fast toward him, still carrying the cup.

He startles but then snarls at me. *"You are done. We will go."*

"Will we now?" I ask as if this is up for debate. I stop just a few feet from him. I only need a couple seconds...

"Yes. Jarod wants you—" The way he flicks a surprised look over my shoulder says my soul mate has come for me.

"Hey, *fuck you!*" I yell, yanking the Vardigah's attention back. Then I splash the poison in his face. He reels back, startled, then he claws at his eyes. A roar behind me makes me jolt, but before I can even react, a *massive thing* is flying over me. I duck down to the floor. A silver, glistening beast that can only be Constantine's dragon sails over my head and lands on the Vardigah, talons first. The technician hardly squeals before those talons finish him, separating his head from his body. I'm huddled on the floor, gaping, as Niko in his fancy fireproof suit hurries up behind me.

He flips his visor up. "You okay?"

I'm all out of words, so I just nod. A split second later, Constantine's silver dragon disappears, and he stands—*naked*—in its place. If I was out of words before, now there's not a thought in my head. Just pure awe at the beauty of the man.

"Where's Sophia?" Niko asks, and it takes me a second to peel my eyes off Constantine's supremely masculine body in order to point to the end of the bookshelves near my cot. Niko trots off.

Constantine strides up to me. "You all right?" he asks, bending down to lift me up to standing. Concern is written all over his face, but he's holding me while completely naked, so once again—no words. I nod fervently, then manage to shut my gaping mouth and swallow.

He slides past me, and my gaze is drawn to watching him go, like a female compass needle to the True North of Manhood. He's just that bloody beautiful. While he hastily slides his clothes back on, I try to come back to my senses.

Niko steps around the corner, carrying Sophia. "I'm taking her." To Constantine, he says, "I'm coming right back. And we need a plan."

"Right."

Niko disappears with Sophia. Constantine's got his trousers on, but he just carries his shirt over to me, still bare-chested. I try not to be dazzled. But then he kisses me—just on the forehead, fast and fierce. It knocks the words out of me again.

"Alice, my love, we've got to figure this out." He releases me then takes hold of my wrist, the one with the X on it. "How can we break this?"

"I don't know." I glare at all the ancient books on my shelves. "None of these say anything about breaking elvish magic."

Constantine lets go of my hand and runs his through his hair. "All I know about the Vardigah is that mated dragon venom is poisonous to them. That's why they hate us. Why they don't want us to mate. Maybe you can guide Niko to their leader—"

"Jarod." But there's something he said…

"*Jarod.* If Niko can kill him, or even threaten him, maybe they will release the hex on you…" He trails off as I'm gravitating to my bookshelves. I remember something… "Alice?"

"You said something…" I trail my finger across the books. *Potions. Casting. Rejuvenation.* "Something about dragons being dangerous to Vardigah."

Constantine follows me as I hunt through the shelves. "Dragon venom. Only mated dragons, though—"

I stop cold and stare at him. "Mated dragons."

"Yes. That's when the venom is activated —what?"

But I'm on a hunt now. *Spells. Physicks. Gardens and Herbs.* "Yes!" *Dragons and their Habits.* I pull it from the shelf and drop it on the workbench with a *thunk.*

Niko reappears a few feet away. "Okay, what's the plan?"

Constantine shrugs.

I'm leafing through the book like mad. "There's something about elvish magic and dragon magic." *Christ, where's the page?* "That they're poisonous to one another. A dragon's bite will kill an elf, but something else…" *I find it.* "Ah!" I start to read. "A mated dragon's form is toxic to the elvish race. In mated form, the bite is poisonous, and *a mated dragon cannot be bound by elvish magic.*" The emphasis is mine. "The two magic systems are incompatible. Elvish magic can destroy a mated dragon, but it cannot put a hold upon the beast." My heart is near bursting from my chest. "Constantine!"

His eyes are wide. "I don't understand—"

"*If we mate,* they cannot bind me."

At first, he's shocked. "My love…" Then he takes hold of my shoulders, illegally sexy in just his fireproof pants and no shirt at all. "Mating takes *time.* Besides, you'd have to be in love with me, or it wouldn't work."

"You foolish man!" I nearly laugh. "What do you think this is all about?"

Now he's the one stunned out of words, but Niko still has them. "Great! So, we need to get you two somewhere where you can get busy and break that fucking elvish tracker. By fucking. Literally. *Constantine!*" He snaps his fingers in Constantine's face. "Tell me you can handle this."

He blinks at Niko. "I... yes." He turns back. "You love me?" He says it like it's some impossible violation of the laws of physics and magic.

"For the love of God, man." I just shake my head. Are they all this clueless?

"Hey," Niko says, brightly. "I know just the place." He lays a hand on my shoulder and the other on Constantine's, who still looks as if he's been hit with a rock on the head. "Are you ready?"

My heart squeezes as I realize—*I'm leaving. And I'm not coming back.* "My books, Niko. And all the supplies. But mostly the books. Whatever you can scamper away with."

He grins. "I'll come back for them."

Then suddenly the workshop disappears, and we're standing beside a cottage that's so lovely, it makes my heart hurt. A green field stretches out from it, and a whisper of wind goes through the trees at the outskirts. In the distance, the wink of light on the loch is a love poem to Ireland all by itself.

It's not the tiny village I grew up in.

But it couldn't feel more like home.

NINE

Constantine

I'VE ARRIVED AT A SMALL SLICE OF HEAVEN.

Niko's dropped us at a fairy tale cottage in what looks like the Irish countryside. Alice—my *soul mate*—is in my arms. I'm half-dressed, and she's looking at me with lust in her eyes. She says she loves me, but my body is strung tight in full panic mode.

Because the Vardigah could burn everything down at any moment.

Just like before, only this time... I know it's coming.

"I'm no expert," she says, splaying her hands across my chest, "but I think you have to *touch me,* Constantine, to mate with me. Or did the books lie about that?" She's *flirting* with me.

It just spins my head more. "They could be here

any moment." I slip my arm around her waist and pull her against me, but I can't help holding her wrist—the one with the mark—where I can see it. We're still outside the cottage. I should take her inside, but I'm frozen. Mechanical. Fucking this up entirely.

"I'll admit," she says softly, running her hands along my chest and up to my cheek. "Not how I imagined this, either."

That pulls me in. I tear my gaze from the mark that holds her captive and peer into those beautiful brown eyes. "You've imagined this? *Us,*" I clarify. "Together?"

"I've had a dream of it," she whispers, her fingertips tracing along my jaw as she looks up at me. "For years now. A vision, really, that you and Cinder and Ember would come and change everything. I didn't know how. Not until Jarod started making me find the women and bring them in. Then I started to plan. And… well…" She brushes her fingers across my lips. "This part was just a wish that this might come before the end of all of it."

She'd planned to die, all along. I can see it now —she never thought she'd get out of this alive. And we still might not. But I'll give her that happy ending even if it is *the end.*

I lean down to kiss her. She opens her mouth, eager but unsure, just like before. I leave her lips to bend down farther and grab hold of her bottom to lift her from her feet. I start walking us to the front door of the cottage.

Her arms are around my neck. "I don't suppose there's a bed in there?" There's excitement in her eyes.

"I'll take you up against the wall if I have to." My cock is already sprung.

She shudders delightfully in my arms, but I have to set her down to open the door. Inside is a tiny front room, but I see the meadow down the hall and through the floor-to-ceiling windows of the bedroom. I drop down to lift her properly this time —skirts hiked up, legs spread, her ankles hooked around my back.

"I like you like this." My voice is getting rougher as I clutch her bottom and carry her toward the bedroom.

That flush of pink is lighting up her cheeks. "You'll have to show me how." She's ducking her head like this embarrasses her.

I nuzzle her cheek. "You'll have to tell me what you like."

She shudders again then tucks her head into the

crook of my neck. I'm honestly worried—Alice has to be a virgin. Or abused. The fucking Vardigah have held her captive since she was seven, and I pray to all that's magic that whatever abuse they've doled out to her wasn't a violation. But it could be. And here I am, having to rush this, just to break her from their grasp... when all I want to do is take my sweet time and gently, carefully, love this gorgeous woman.

The bed is perfectly white—pillows and covers, with lace everywhere. This must be a honeymooner cottage for the mated dragons, although I've never paid attention to that before. But it has the look—a large playground of a bed, a gorgeous view, the solitude of no neighbors within sight.

I carry Alice into the bed, only setting her down when I can cover her body with mine. Her hands go into my hair, and I kiss her deeply. Her body's already arching into mine, even though I'm pressing us both into the firmness of the bed.

I pull back and gaze down at her. "We don't have much time."

She grins. "Then why are you wasting it with words?"

"I need you to know, I *would* take my time. We would go slow and careful and any... *pain*... you might carry would be kissed away a thousand times before I even—" Her fingers on my lips stop me.

"I love your words, Constantine." Her face is flushed. Her eyes dilated. "But it's not your words I need right now."

Fuck. Me. "Then I'll give you what you need." I cover her mouth with mine and kiss her long and deep, my body skimming hers. She has way too many clothes on, and I'm not taking time to fix that. My hands find her breasts through the dress, kneading and aching to uncover them. All that will have to wait. I lean back, leaving her splayed on the bed, arms fallen back and resting on either side of her head. Her gorgeous red hair is spilled all over the white bedspread, and her lips are parted, slightly swollen from our kissing.

I sit up on my knees and tear at the fasteners for my pants. In a second, I've got that shoved down to my knees, freeing my cock, which is fully at attention and ready for her. She lifts up on her elbows, and her stare for it is shocked and slightly alarmed.

Fuck. If the mere sight of a cock is freaking her out... "You okay?"

She visibly swallows. "I wasn't expecting that."

"You weren't expecting me to be a man?" I grin, but it's a relief—if she's *surprised* that means she's just inexperienced, not abused. At least not in that way.

"Wasn't expecting it to be so *big.*"

My grin goes wide—I lean forward, covering her again, my cock pressing against her skirt as I slide up to give her a quick kiss. "Are you flattering me for some reason, Alice?" I say, copying her words and accent as best I can.

"Just stating the obvious." But she has a laugh back in her eyes.

I kiss her again, softly. "I aim to give you nothing but pleasure," I whisper. "But if it hurts, you need to tell me."

She grabs my face with both hands. "I belong to you, Constantine." She pulls me into another kiss, longer and deeper. The truth of that—of her *love* for me, which I still can't believe—sends a tremor through me. She's my second chance. My one and only, forever. If these next moments are all we have —if the Vardigah come to slay us in our mating bed —we will have at least gotten *here.*

To this moment.

I finish the kiss because I have so much more I want to do. I lean back again and slide her skirt up her legs. She's watching me, eyes still wide. Most of the fabric is her cloak, which is under her now—

her dress is lightweight and bunches easily up to her waist. Underneath are her panties. I want to spend *lots* of time here, but I only have a little. I give a gentle kiss to the delicate skin of her thigh as I lift her bottom to edge the panties down. She gives that delightful shudder again, and I can't resist. I kiss my way to the heat between her legs, tasting her and giving her a preview of what I'd like to do.

She gasps and grabs at my head. *"Fuck, yes!"*

Well, hell... I double down on that, lapping and licking her into more cursing and bucking. Then she starts this delicious whimper, and I'm *so* tempted to make her come, right now, with just the tip of my tongue... but we need to *mate*. That means magic I can't just coax out with my mouth. It's not a one-sided giving of pleasure—although, *fuck me*, I want to do this all day long. But if there's one thing I viscerally understand, it's the proper order of things.

I stop that delicious torment and slide my body along hers, lining my aching cock up with her now thoroughly-wet entrance. "I need to be inside you, my love," I whisper. We have to come together to bond, to fuse the two halves of the souls that we've been carrying for centuries.

"Oh, fuck yes," she breathes, grabbing at my shoulders and pulling me closer.

I take hold of her wrists and pin them to the bed. The Vardigah's X is blaring at me, an inky reminder we haven't any time at all. I ease the tip of my cock inside and watch her eyes go wide and her mouth open in surprise. I slip out then back in a little farther. *Holy fuck*, she's tight.

"Relax, my love," I whisper, dropping kisses on her lips while her mouth gapes open. "We'll take it slow."

She takes a deep breath and lets it out in one long sigh.

"You all right?" I ask as I pull out and sink a little deeper back in.

She sucks in air again. "Yes. Oh, yes." She finds my gaze. "Take me all the way."

I hesitate, but she has that blazing determination I love dancing in her eyes. This time, when I stroke in, I don't stop until I'm all the way seated, even as she arches and calls out my name and gasps her way through it.

I hold still. She sinks back into the bed. I bend to nuzzle her cheek. I'm not even close to done, but I'm as deep into my soul mate as I can go. We're as tightly joined as it's possible for two people to be.

And while the desire to thrust is almost overwhelming, the ancient words float up in my mind and trickle out of my lips.

"You complete me, Alice O'Rourke," I whisper, cheek to cheek. "Your soul is my soul. Your heart beats with mine. You are the greatest treasure I will ever have."

When I lift my head, there's a shine in her eyes. "Not time nor land…" She waits for me.

"Nor sea contain," I say, pulling back and then thrusting back in.

She gasps as I land. "Nor death nor life…"

"Nor soul remain." My heart is soaring as my body moves.

"When two hearts beat…" She arches up into my thrust.

"Their broke," I grind out as I thrust harder, "souls cry."

"Ever more." She whimpers as I take her. *"Now."* And I think she means it. That she's close.

I don't want to finish the verse. I want to keep thrusting until she comes.

But I say it anyway, between jolts of pleasure ripping through us both. *"Till now,"* I gasp, *"they die."* I groan and bury my face in her neck. She's crying out as I thrust, each one higher as we race together. My entire body tightens. *"My love, my love,"* I pant.

"Constantine!" she cries, then she convulses under me. I feel her body clutch tight around me, and that pulls me over the edge. I'm still holding her wrists pinned to the bed, buried deep as I empty myself into her, wave after crashing wave of pleasure. Her cries and whimpers settle just as my cascade of pleasure finally ends. I'm panting, my head tucked against hers, suddenly wiped of all tension, all thought.

I stay joined with her—honestly, I can't even contemplate leaving her body, ever—but I release the death-grip I've had on her hands. Belatedly, I fear I might have hurt her. I pull back and cup her cheek. Her eyes are closed, and I know that look—that's a woman well pleasured. And it brings me the kind of joy I've seldom experienced: deep and resonant, like my whole body might lift straight off the bed with the brilliance of it. This isn't manly pride, this is pure, transcendent love.

I kiss her cheek. Then her lips. She hardly moves.

I grin. "Are you all right there?" I tease.

"I just need a moment for what's happening in my body."

I smile because I think she means the pleasure we've just wrenched out of each other, but then I glance at the Vardigah mark...

And it's gone.

"Alice," I gasp.

Her eyes are still closed "How do you live after feeling like this?" She sleepily opens her eyes. "How do you go back to just having an ordinary day?"

My smile might break me. "We're mated." Then I realize... "Do you feel it?" I put my hand to her cheek and sure enough—she's burning up. The heat of the transformation is already happening.

She blinks more awake. "I feel hot. And like your cock might have been the death of me."

I scowl and look down where we're still joined. "Are you hurt?"

"Oh, there's a soreness, for sure."

I grimace and ease out. Alice moans through it, and not in a good way. "My love, I'm so sorry." I cuddle up to her, stroking her hair, my touch as light as I can make it.

She's staring at her wrist, where the X used to be. "It worked. Fucking amazing."

"So, it was worth the pain?"

She turns her gaze to me. "Oh, *that* was worth the pain even if I still carried the mark."

I grin, and I'm tingly all over with the realization: *we're free.* We've broken free of the Vardigah, everyone is safe, and I have newly-mated Alice in my bed. I take another moment to realize the tingle is something *real.* I've come into my powers as a mated dragon.

"Well, now that we have more time..." I sit up and grasp her arm—the one now free of the Vardigah's mark—and pull her up to sitting. "Exactly how do I get you out of this dress?"

A slow, sexy smile blooms on her face.

I've never seen anything so hot in my life.

TEN

Alice

THE WIND IS SIGHING, THE SUN IS BRILLIANT WARM, and the breeze is just right on my backside.

And Constantine is taking me up against a tree *hard*, just like he promised.

"Oh, baby... *fuck*," he says, and I agree.

So much fucking.

We've been at it nearly nonstop since the beginning. I was a bit sore at first, but Constantine explained the unnatural powers of a mated dragon, notably for healing, and how it wasn't just the talent of his tongue that had me feeling absolutely no pain after that first bit.

Although his tongue is, without question, a magical artifact of its own.

I have to shift my grip on the tree. I'm bent over,

arms outstretched, fingers digging into the bark. Only I'm still adjusting to my new strength, and I keep crushing the bark right off the tree. But the feel of Constantine—hard and thick and long—taking me from behind, is worth the fact that I can barely hold on through the thrusting.

"Is this what you wanted?" he pants.

"Mm, hmm. *Ung.*" That's all I can manage between whimpers.

But I love that he keeps checking on me. Making sure everything's just right. I love every bit about this man, but that's the most amazing thing to me—as I've not had anything like it most of my life.

"Ok, my love. But I really need you like this." He pulls out and turns me, bringing me up into his arms. He kisses me deep then reaches down to lift me off my feet. I think maybe he's going to take me like this—just legs dangling in the air as he raises and lowers me on his cock—but instead, he walks us back to the tree and sets me on my feet. Well, one foot—the other he's hiked over his hip as he eases into me again. We're technically up against the tree, but his hand is behind my head, protecting it from the roughness of the bark, and his grip on the back of my knee keeps my bare bottom from scraping.

It's just a tiny thing, this consideration. But it fills my entire world. That, and he's rubbing up against my most sensitive parts.

"Do you like that?" he asks as he works me.

Like it? "You're doing all sorts of things to me right now." I moan against his arm, the one protecting me from the tree.

"Good." He grinds against me, making me yelp, then he thrusts again. "Because I can't... *fuck. Alice.*"

"Ah, don't stop," I beg. My fingers are digging into him now, with those broad shoulders even more muscled given he's come into his own powers.

"Come for me," he pants, stepping up the thrusting. And just when I think I can't, he changes his angle, thrusting *up* more, and suddenly I feel it coming. That glorious shock wave that starts between my legs but rockets through my entire body. It's building, and something about the fresh air and the sun and the glorious beauty of the world makes it even more magical.

I cry out his name as it seizes hold of me, pulsing pleasure that convulses my entire being. He does the same, gripping me hard. Deep inside, I feel him, twitching and spilling that seed that one day will make us a baby. A magical baby. A magic dragon-witch baby.

I don't tell him this. I don't know if he's thought of it.

But I see this vision every time he comes hot inside me.

And it's a wondrous thing, too.

Not as wondrous as the sex, though, because that's insane. This lovemaking is a gift from heaven that I almost missed. It's a true miracle that either of us are standing here against a tree, loving anyone, much less each other.

Soul mate. I hadn't even conceived of such a thing for myself. And yet here I am.

"Oh, *fuck*, you were right." He doesn't make any kind of motion to leave the tree.

"Was I?" I toy with his long hair, hanging between us.

His head rests heavy on his arm, bracing us both. "Outdoors is definitely better."

"Glad you could manage it," I tease, running a hand along the sculpted muscles of his chest.

He pulls back and gives me a dirty look. "Was there some doubt?"

"None at all." I smirk.

"Arg, you..." He pulls me away from the tree,

spins me, then hoists me up, so my legs are locked around his waist. He carries me away from the edge of the forest, through the field.

"I feel like I should prove to you just how much I can *manage*," he says.

"What a terrible thing that would be." The steady grind of his firm muscles between my legs makes want to whimper. I manage to hold it in.

He chuckles, deep in his chest, as he's carrying me back toward the cottage. His hands move my bottom, up and down, just a little as we walk. The friction is nearly unbearable. I bite my lip, determined not to let him know how unbelievably *good* it feels.

"Are we going back to check on Niko?" I ask in a determinedly normal voice.

"Nope."

We *had* taken a pause, early on, to let Niko know that we'd mated—and we were free of the Vardigah. He said everyone else was safe as well.

"Are we after some tea?" I ask, but the rhythmic bumping of this walk is making it impossible to keep my voice *normal*.

"Not yet."

We're nearly back. I have no idea what he has planned. It doesn't matter in the slightest. Whatever this man wants, he's my ride until the end—in all the possible meanings of that.

"What on earth… will we do with ourselves then?" The grinding and bumping are getting away from me. I can feel the quiver building.

"We're going to find out how many orgasms I can *manage* to give my mate." Then he picks up the pace on the jostling and the grinding like he intended it all along.

We don't even reach the back steps before I'm crying out and convulsing against his chest, my legs shaking and my hands clawing his back. He holds me tight through it, letting me ride out the storm, petting my hair and growling deep and sexy throughout.

When it passes, and I can breathe again, he simply says, "One."

And he carries me inside.

ELEVEN

Constantine

I THINK WE MIGHT LIVE HERE.

Alice is out in the field, bounding around in her new dragon form. There's no one to see, so she's free to play, and watching the sun glint off her silver scales is like having a dream with my eyes wide open. I'd be out with her except Niko wants to talk. I haven't told him—or Alice—that even though we've only been here a week, we'll probably never leave. He'll need to find another honeymoon cottage for the newly mated dragons in his lair.

Although it sounds like he'll need a dozen.

"Silver dragon, huh?" Niko's back from the kitchen with a beer for himself and one for me.

I take it from him. "We're one spirit, remember?" Silver dragons are rare, but not unheard of.

We're no different from the others, although silver and gold are much like the flowing red hair of my mate—pretty, a little exotic, and not as common as the blackscales.

"Sure, but I'd forgotten *you* were a silverscale." He takes a sip. "Haven't seen your dragon form in forever." He gives me a sideways look.

Not since the fire, probably. I sigh and smile. "I hear I'm not the only one whose heart is healed. How's Grigore doing?"

Niko's eyebrows lift. "It's the craziest thing. I brought Sophia back, but of course, she wasn't paired—and we didn't want to interrupt *you two...*" He glances out at the low-soaring form of my mate, gliding along the meadow flowers. "Really glad for you two, by the way."

"Me too." I grin and take a drink of my beer.

"Anyway," he continues, "Sophia was in bad shape. We had her down in the hospice for the first few days. Then she starts to do better, taking walks around the ward. She just wanders into Grigore's room and strikes up a conversation."

"Did she know? That he was her mate?"

"She says no." Niko shrugs. "I think there's more that draws us than we think."

"Makes sense to me." I set my beer down. I'm

somewhat permanently buzzed on my new life with Alice—the last thing I need is more euphoria. "So how did they figure it out?"

"Here's the weird part," Niko says. "Grigore starts to get *better*. Before they kissed. Long before they mated. He just starts to… come back to life."

I nod. Doesn't seem strange at all. Alice changed me long before we took that sudden leap of faith into mating. "She's his soul mate." I shrug. Seems self-explanatory.

"I guess." He shakes his head and looks out at the meadow. "They're off somewhere in Europe right now, honeymooning. South of France, I think. Complete recovery, according to Grigore."

"He would know." But it makes me happy. Grigore and I scouted and seduced hundreds of women together, and it almost broke the man. It would have broken me, eventually, but I was already a mess. "What's the count now?"

"Mated dragons?" Niko shrugs. "Hard to keep up. Plus everyone's scattered all over. Now that Alice has paired those last seven, there will be even more. Thanks for that, by the way. I hated to intrude on your honeymoon."

I nod my head to Alice in the field. "She was happy to do it." She's back to human now, naked, strolling through the grass. It looks like she's making a wreath of flowers for her hair. Which makes me think of the last time she did that... and how pretty she looked while I took her in the grass. The woman is endlessly perfect for me... I need to cut this visit with Niko short. "So, everyone's set now?"

"For the moment," he says. "We've got rogue dragons coming in, though—the word is getting around that we've got a witch up at the North Lair, and even the dragons who've left our world behind are returning. They want to know who their real soul mates are."

"Just give us a little notice before you pop in, okay?"

Niko chuckles. "They can wait a little longer." Then he gets serious again. "Things are kind of a mess, though."

"How's that?" Seems to me like everything's just about perfect.

He lists them off. "It took a while, but Saryn and Julia are finally mated, so that's good. Most of the dragons that Alice paired with women on the outside—not captured by the Vardigah—are off to romance their mates."

I smile. "They'll have to return to the old ways."

"Except it's not fucking 1820 anymore." Niko scowls.

"Shouldn't that make it easier?" I lift an eyebrow. "They've been romancing women all along, Niko, just like me. Have they forgotten everything overnight?"

"Well, *yes*, actually." He looks amazingly frustrated for something that should be working just fine. "It's one thing to romance a woman for a night, on the million-to-one odds that she's your mate. It's another thing entirely when you *know* she's your mate, your one fucking chance on this planet to get this right in this lifetime, and she doesn't swipe right on your Tinder."

I grimace. "Ouch."

"Yeah." He sighs. "I'm running a full-time counseling service out of my office. And then there are the women who were tortured by the Vardigah." He shakes his head. "Most of them are seriously traumatized. The same kind of soul-sickness that Cinder had only it's manifesting in different ways with each of them. Some are sticking it out, letting their mates help with the healing. But some want nothing to do with anything magic. A few have already left."

"Where did they go?" I'm assuming Niko has someone watching over them.

"Back to New York City."

That's not good. "And their mates?"

"Still figuring it out."

I nod. "There's still hope, then."

"That's true. We've never had more hope for dragonkind than we do right now." He turns with a real smile. "Ember wants to know if you're doing your part to increase the dragon race."

"Just because you two are overachievers—"

He throws up his hands. "It's not my fault she's pregnant with twins already."

I laugh outright. "Well, it better be!"

He shrugs, but I can see the pride—and he's earned it. He's been the steadying force through all of this, from the darkest days right after the fire, all the way through rescuing twenty-five mates from the Vardigah.

Twenty-six. With my Alice being the biggest prize.

She's out in the middle of the field wearing only a crown of flowers.

"*Niko...*" I say.

"Yeah, I know. I'm leaving." He sets down his beer.

I tear my gaze from the meadow. *"We're* not. Ever. This is our home now."

"All right, then." But he nods like he approves.

"You can come by anytime. *Text first,* for fuck's sake." I point to Alice in the meadow. "But she'll want to be your dragon matchmaker. She says it's her purpose. It's in her blood. And I fully intend to give that woman everything she wants in this world, including the ability to bring a little more love into it."

Niko claps his hand on my shoulder. "Spoken like a true soul mate." Then he releases me, smiles, and teleports away.

I gaze out at the lovely vision awaiting me in the meadow. I could teleport out there. I could take her by surprise. But instead, I take my time, saunter through the grass, enjoy the view, and savor the knowledge that I'm the luckiest damn dragon on the planet.

I get to make love to this woman all the days of my life.

Want to know what Alisa's releasing next?

Subscribe to Alisa's newsletter

for new releases and giveaways

http://smarturl.it/AWsubscribeBARDS

About the Author

Alisa Woods lives in the Midwest with her husband and family, but her heart will always belong to the beaches and mountains where she grew up. She writes sexy paranormal romances about complicated men and the strong women who love them. Her books explore the struggles we all have, where we resist—and succumb to—our most tempting vices as well as our greatest desires. No matter the challenge, Alisa firmly believes that hearts can mend and love will triumph over all.

www.AlisaWoodsAuthor.com